AF084320

Masks of Illusion

by

TK Orbelyan

ISBN: 978-1-916732-17-9

Also by TK Orbelyan

Fangs of Deception

Copyright 2024

All rights reserved. No part of this publication may be reproduced, stored in a retrieval system, or transmitted in any form or by any means, electronic, mechanical, photocopy, recording or otherwise, without prior written consent of the copyright owner. Nor can it be circulated in any form of binding or cover other than that in which it is published and without similar condition including this condition being imposed on a subsequent purchaser. The right of T K Orbelyan to be identified as the author of this work has been asserted in accordance with the Copyright Designs and Patents Act 1988. A copy of this book is deposited with the British Library.

i2i Publishing. Manchester.
www.i2ipublishing.co.uk

The most dangerous prison
is inside our minds.

Chapter One

It was a warm and quiet spring morning, with the countryside around Birch Heights emitting fewer sounds than it usually did at that time of day. Terry and Emily had come up with the name a few weeks after moving to their new home — a converted barn near the village of Cudworth in Somerset. It sat close to the top of a hill overlooking a picturesque valley dotted with elms and cypresses and had two large birch trees standing alongside it like twin sentinels.

Emily, who was playing in the garden with Ollie, heard her brother's car approaching before she saw it. As it neared the house, she stood up and shielded her eyes from the bright sun. She was looking forward to seeing Alan again. Their last meeting had been at Christmas in Frome, when he and Tracey had finally announced a date for their wedding. It would be in the summer, with a small service in the local chapel being followed by a romantic ceremony at a country estate near Blagdon that boasted a vineyard and a rich collection of delectable wines. Their engagement had lasted almost four years, and everyone in the Turnbull family was delighted that Tracey would soon be a formal part of it.

Alan parked on the gravel path in front of the garden and jumped out. Shylock—Terry's and Emily's black and white springer spaniel—ran up to him with a tennis ball in his mouth, which Alan threw towards the birch trees for him to fetch.

"Hi sis, how's our little champ doing?"

Oliver—or Ollie as everyone called him—was now seventeen months old and was developing into a boisterous little boy with a contagious laugh.

Alan bent down and picked him up, lifting him up above his head and moving him horizontally from side to side in a gliding motion. Ollie giggled uncontrollably. Emily gave her brother a warm hug. She and Alan had always been close, and she deeply appreciated the help he had given her and Terry when they had first moved to the barn house. He had also spent a lot of time with them when Ollie was born, in contrast to her two sisters, who had offered only token assistance.

Terry appeared at the door and smiled at his brother-in-law.

"Been a while, Alan. Don't make yourself a stranger around here. We live in the same county, after all."

They shook hands and sat down on the deckchairs on the porch while Emily lay down on the grass and resumed the game she had been playing with Ollie.

"This setting's so ideal for bringing up a child, isn't it?" Alan remarked as he made himself comfortable. "I can see how happy Ollie is here."

"Yep, moving out of London was the right thing to do, no doubt about it," Emily concurred.

"I love watching him run around barefoot on the grass, enjoying the sunshine and breathing in plenty of fresh air. Now that spring has arrived, we're trying to spend most of the day outdoors."

"And so you should. Somerset is enchanting this time of year."

"I love it throughout the year," Emily said gleefully, "but yes, springtime is gorgeous. We go down to the stream almost every day. Ollie loves splashing about in the water in his wellies."

Shylock returned with the ball and dropped it in Alan's lap. Alan pretended to throw it a few times, finding Shylock's confused stare highly amusing. He finally threw it as far as he could and watched as the sprightly creature sprinted off after it.

"I remember how excited you both were when you first bought this house. I wasn't sure you'd be able to live off-grid like this, but you've surprised me. And you've taught me an important lesson — that it's not just *possible* but even preferable to live without TV, generate your own electricity and make do without gas."

"It's been tough at times," Emily noted, "especially during the really cold months, but otherwise it's been fantastic. The only thing we missed desperately when we came here was the internet, which is why we arranged for a phone line to be connected to the house a month after moving in. Other than that, we've lived perfectly well, and very frugally."

Terry went into the kitchen and came back with three ginger ales. "How's the restaurant doing?"

The recession that had begun at the end of 2022 was now in its third year, and Frome—like most towns and cities across the country—had seen shops and small businesses collapse one after the other. Alan's seafood restaurant had survived, though, but only just, a fact he attributed to his stellar reputation and excellent customer reviews. However, 2025 was promising to be just as challenging financially as the previous two years had been, with few signs that economic activity in the UK was about to pick up.

"I'm hanging on. The fact that so many other restaurants have closed down recently means that competition is less, but the real problem is the lack of spending power. Everyone's skint."

"Yes, of course," agreed Terry, "but that's what they've wanted to do all along — drive people into a precarious existence, crash the economy, digitise all money and get rid of cash. Then, everything will be set for their blasted social credit system to be unleashed."

"You'll be glad to know I've put up a sign on the door that says WE PROUDLY ACCEPT CASH. It's actually helped business quite a bit because many of our customers — especially the older ones — prefer to pay in cash. Those places that stopped accepting cash have really shot themselves in the foot. But one man's folly is another man's fortune, I guess... not that I'm making a fortune, but at least I'm hanging on."

Alan knew that one of the campaigns Terry and Emily had been active in over the last year was the movement to keep cash alive, despite the government's stringent efforts to make businesses prioritise digital forms of payment. It was abundantly clear to them that the phasing out of cash was designed to eliminate personal privacy and usher in the age of social credit scores along the lines of what China had been doing for close to a decade. In their eyes, this move was amongst the most threatening to human freedoms of all the nefarious measures that had been taken since 2019 under the guise of a global pandemic. As Terry kept reminding people, not only would it harm millions of small traders and freelance workers doing odd jobs, it would also allow the government to shut off people's money digitally whenever they stepped out of line.

"Well done," Terry grinned. "You've finally come round to doing it. What took you so long?"

"I know! I should have put it up months ago. The issue now is how long they'll allow me to accept cash before they ban it outright. How long do you think we've got?"

"Not long. These miscreants want to wrap things up by the end of the decade at the latest, so cash transactions will probably be made illegal sometime within the next couple of years, I'd say."

"Blimey, I hope you're wrong. The thought of not being able to buy anything without having my name and details registered somewhere is horrifying."

"It's not just the loss of privacy that's an issue," said Emily. "Having only digital money will mean you won't be able to contest fines, taxes or any other charges before paying them. They'll just deduct the amount automatically from your digital account without you even knowing it. You'll wake up in the morning and discover you were fined overnight and have already paid for it. And if you were planning to buy something essential that day but the money's not in your account any more, too bad…"

"That's exactly what the Chinese have been facing for years," Terry added, "but they've got it even worse. They actually have to *earn* social credits by being good citizens and ratting on their neighbours; and if they misbehave — for example by demonstrating against a government decision or writing something critical on social media — they lose points. Once you lose a certain number of points, you cannot access government services or buy railway or airline tickets. You're effectively banned from moving around. That's why instead of calling it digital money, we should really be calling it *programmable* money, because governments can programme every aspect of your life through it. They can even give your money an expiry date — if you don't spend an X amount of money in your digital account by so-and-so date, it'll expire and you won't have it anymore. I can't think of a better way of preventing people from saving, can you? Digital money will be nothing short of a tracking and control system once cash is gone."

"It's hard to imagine the British people accepting something like that, though, isn't it?" said Alan, trying to sound optimistic.

"Five years ago it was hard to imagine that more than two-thirds of the country would agree to get jabbed with an experimental concoction that had no safety or efficacy data, and yet it happened. Three years ago, it was hard to imagine that everyone would accept a huge increase in energy costs just to punish Russia, but *that* happened too. You see, when they take the final step and remove all cash from the economy, they'll sweeten it by rolling out something like universal basic income to fool people. Millions of people struggling financially will be overjoyed at the idea of receiving a monthly income for doing nothing, and they'll gladly accept the new system. This isn't a conspiracy theory; they've been piloting universal basic income in different parts of England since 2023. I remember seeing it being trialled in East Finchley just before we moved out here."

Alan shrugged forlornly. He knew Terry was right. "I suppose this system will pave the way for a single global currency too."

"Most definitely," said Terry. "It'll probably be national digital currencies first, created by each country's central bank, and then the different currencies will be merged into one. Once you have a global currency, there's no such thing as exchange rates anymore, which means you can digitally create as much money as you want without the currency crashing, and production will be moved away from industrialised countries to regions of the world with the lowest salaries and safety rules — a literal race to the bottom. Trade deficits between countries won't matter, since for all intents and purposes, the global economy will be a single market, with the regions suffering massive de-industrialisation being unable to take any measures to stop the slide. You'll just see mass movements of people."

"We're seeing it already, mate," Alan responded. "I can't believe how severely some parts of the UK have been de-industrialised. We hardly manufacture anything anymore. Gone are the days when we actually *made* things in this country."

"Germany has suffered even worse than we have, but they got the brunt of the energy crisis from the Ukraine war. And, of course, they had their energy pipeline blown up."

"That's true," Alan agreed, "and there's no doubt that jobs are disappearing fast, but curiously the unemployment rate hasn't skyrocketed. Are they faking the statistics, do you think?"

"Most likely, but then again, we've had the phenomenon of 'excess deaths' since 2021, haven't we? Hundreds of thousands of them. Over four years, that adds up to quite a lot…"

Alan understood that Terry was referring to the UK's unnaturally high death rate. While the government was doing its best to hide the true picture, anecdotal evidence was showing a steady decline in the country's population. The most shocking data was the number of stillbirths and miscarriages, which had shot up since the roll-out of the vaccines, and yet not a single mainstream media outlet had deemed it important enough to mention.

"Some whistleblowers told us this was going to happen, but nobody listened to them," Terry continued. "They said we were going to see a massive spike in unexplained deaths as soon as needles started going into people's arms. They also said that depopulation would primarily come from the loss of fertility and the inability to carry a pregnancy to full term. Sadly, they were absolutely right."

Emily took Ollie into her arms and squeezed him. She knew how lucky she was to have been able to have a child. Several of her friends were trying to have a baby but had had repeated miscarriages.

"What on earth can we do about the move to digitalise all money?" Alan asked, returning to the earlier topic of conversation.

"I've come up with an idea," said Terry. "One way of circumventing it and retaining a certain degree of privacy in transactions is through bartering, which is the world's oldest form of trade. I'm thinking of setting up an online platform where people can anonymously post goods and services they want to exchange for other goods and services. For example, a home decorator may agree to repaint a piano teacher's home in exchange for lessons for his daughter, or a plumber might fix someone's toilet in return for fresh produce or some other item. The key is to create a large online community of people who are keen on bartering and to facilitate transactions between them. Users can list all the goods and services they want to offer and post whatever it is they need. They'll also have ratings for punctuality, quality of service, and so on. Once two users are interested in making a transaction, they'll be able to chat with each other anonymously, and it will then be up to them to decide whether they want to actually contact each other outside of the platform to complete their transaction."

"I like it," Alan said. "I can definitely see it taking off, but how would the platform make money?"

"There'd have to be a small membership fee, payable quarterly or bi-yearly."

"It says a lot about the times we're living in that we're even having such a discussion," Alan said with a dry smile. "The fact that we need to think of ways to barter things because using cash won't be allowed…"

"Indeed," Terry said. "Ours was pretty much the last generation that grew up without smart technology and artificial intelligence. We are the last generation—at least in the West—who experienced privacy and personal freedom."

Emily nodded gloomily. "Yes, the world we grew up in is well and truly gone. Healthy non-GMO food, skies without chemtrails, no compulsory IDs, no CCTV everywhere. Hardly anything of that world will remain when this dystopia finally comes about. Just an echo…"

"There's a Welsh word that describes perfectly what you mean," Alan said. "*Hiraeth*. It signifies a spiritual longing for the lost world of the past, which now exists only in the wind, in the rocks and the waves. It's a nostalgia for a home we cannot return to, a home we yearn for, but also a home which maybe never existed. We may have imagined it existed because the world around us allowed us to imagine it, but it may have always been an illusion."

Terry pondered on what Alan had just said. Was this emerging dystopia they were living in always there, just under the surface? Was the old world they all remembered so fondly nothing more than an illusion? He didn't know the answer.

Chapter Two

Terry took his time as he drove down the winding gravel road leading from the barn house to the main road. He always enjoyed reading the road names he had given to each separate stretch of the road between curves. When they had first moved to their new home, he had told Emily about his idea to add name posts honouring whistleblowers and truth-tellers whom—by and large—the public had never heard about, but she had responded laconically. She didn't think highly of such gestures, but she didn't necessarily disapprove of them either. So, within months of settling in, Terry had made several wooden signposts and placed them along different stretches of the gravel road. Due to the remoteness of the area, no one had said anything, and he hadn't been told to remove them, a fact he had found quite surprising.

The first stretch was called Jim Garrison Road, in honour of the District Attorney who had launched the only prosecution ever against organisers of the assassination of President John F. Kennedy. Another section was called Bill Cooper Road, in memory of the American whistleblower who had revealed some of the US government's secrets about its contacts with extraterrestrials and whose book *Behold a Pale Horse* became a cult classic. The last section was called Dolores Cannon Road, in homage to the hypnotherapist and psychic whose works on reincarnation and the interconnectedness between all living creatures in the universe had resonated with him so profoundly when he had first delved into the field of human consciousness. Cannon's books had been amongst his bestsellers at Barricade Books in the genre of spirituality, and he had read all thirteen of her works.

As he left the gravel road, he felt satisfaction at his commemoration of such individuals, with whom he felt a deep connection. He stepped on the accelerator and drove off, not wanting to be late for his meeting. He was on the way to Monmouth in Wales to take part in a video recording for Richard Andrews' documentary channel. Richard and he had become good friends following Carl's untimely demise, and he appreciated the help and support Richard had offered him and his family. Over the last year and a half, he had attended most of Richard's events and had become an avid follower of his work. During many lengthy discussions, he had also revealed to Richard the research he himself had conducted on certain topics, some of which revolved around the pandemic psyop. It had therefore not come as a huge surprise to him when Richard had invited him at the start of the year to take part in a panel discussion on the JFK assassination, secret societies and the infiltration of governments by non-human entities. The other interviewee would be Derek Johnson, who was well known in truther circles for his work on animal mutilations, human abductions and UFO cover-ups.

Over the previous three years, Terry had studied the Kennedy assassination extensively and was highly knowledgeable about the subject. Although he was looking forward to the discussion, he was also slightly nervous about appearing on Richard's channel. Ever since becoming part of the truther movement, he had done his research quietly and unobtrusively. He and Emily had always suspected that their phone in their flat in Islington had been bugged and that that was how Raul had known about Emily being pregnant before anyone else. He therefore believed that he was on somebody's radar, or at least had been, but he had hoped that moving away and keeping a low profile would have caused those people—whoever they were—to look elsewhere and forget about him. Now, with this panel discussion, he knew his activities would come under the spotlight again, but even though he understood what the implications of going ahead with it could be, he had decided that he would either be fully in the movement or out of it.

Emily had been supportive of his decision, albeit from a different angle. Her belief had been that appearing in one of Richard Andrews' programmes wouldn't make that much of a difference in terms of the authorities finding out about people such as them, since they probably knew already – through infiltrators or surveillance – who attended protest meetings and who was active in the movement. Her only warning had been for Terry to be somewhat reserved when expressing his personal views, which she knew could occasionally sound excessively conspiratorial.

Terry arrived in Monmouth around 10:30am and made his way to Richard's studio. Derek Johnson was already there and the three of them discussed the programme's schedule over some coffee. Terry had met Derek once before at one of Richard's presentations, but their conversation had been brief. Derek had made a very good impression on him, and he was looking forward to learning more about cattle mutilations and human abductions, topics that interested him hugely.

Recording began at 11:30am, with Richard giving a brief introduction of the two guests and starting the discussion with Derek, who began by describing what was meant by the term 'animal mutilations'.

"For several decades now," he stated bluntly, "farm animals across Britain have been found horrifically mutilated, with the nature of the mutilations fitting a very specific and easily recognisable pattern. This phenomenon is happening in a host of countries, but for some unexplained reason it seems to be more prevalent in the UK and North America. The animals are typically cows, horses, sheep and goats, but on rare occasions, other animals—including bulls, household pets and even seals—have been found dead with similar wounds. The commonalities between all of the documented cases include the complete lack of blood in and around the carcass, the surgical removal of certain organs and glands, the removal of part of the facial tissue around the mouth, anal coring, and evidence that the animals have been dropped from a height following their deaths."

Terry was listening intently. He had heard of this peculiar yet horrific phenomenon but had never studied it in depth.

"What sort of response has there been from the government and the mainstream media to such occurrences?" Richard asked Derek.

"Almost invariably their response is to explain away such occurrences as normal animal predation or the work of satanists engaging in animal sacrifice. However, both explanations are false. Numerous experts have told me that the mutilations could not have been the result of animal predation, and the fact that not a single animal-sacrifice ritual has ever been seen at the site of these mutilations rules out the satanist explanation. I'd like to see how a group of people could hold down a 2,000-pound bull in the dark and drain it of blood while coring its back end..."

Terry chuckled at the image. Surely nobody in their right mind would ever approach a live bull with the intention of mutilating it, he thought.

"Who do *you* think is behind these mutilations?" Richard asked finally.

Derek didn't mince his words. "I have spoken to several farmers and ranchers in both the UK and the US who have seen their farm animals either lifted into or dropped from a craft hovering above their property. I can also confirm that video footage exists of this happening, and I have seen some of it.

"My conclusion is that animal mutilations that fit the aforementioned pattern are not the work of human beings, but governments are doing their best to give prosaic explanations for the phenomenon to cover up what's really going on."

Richard thanked him for sharing his insights and turned to Terry, saying that the Kennedy assassination—though a subject that had been investigated and researched doggedly for decades—was still very topical and relevant to the crises facing humanity at the present time. With that, he handed over to Terry, who began outlining the main theories surrounding the motives for the assassination. He started with the revelation that JFK had been moving to break up the CIA, and stated his belief that the intelligence agency had likely conspired to have him killed. He then spoke about the hatred that many foreign-policy hardliners had for Kennedy, especially after the failed Bay of Pigs invasion, and explored the notion that the assassination had been orchestrated by certain elements in the military-industrial complex. The next theory he examined was that of the Mafia being involved, and showed how Kennedy's brother Robert, who was Attorney General at the time, had launched a relentless crusade against organised crime, which had seen an 800 per cent increase in convictions and had provoked the ire of the head of the FBI, who himself had long been suspected of having mob ties. He discussed how it was very likely that the mob *had* been involved in the plot to assassinate Kennedy, but only in a minor or supportive capacity.

Finally, he discussed the theory that had been examined the least by historians—that the assassination had been carried out to prevent Kennedy from revealing details about the US government's dealings with non-human entities. To make his point, he quoted from a famous interview Bill Cooper had given in which he had claimed that just days before the assassination, Kennedy had instructed NASA and other agencies to reveal everything they knew about UFO crashes, contact with ETs, and back-engineered alien technology. He said that even though there were many individuals who wanted JFK dead, this lead was arguably the most promising in terms of shedding light on the real culprits, and that the organisers most likely included elements from all of the aforementioned agencies and organisations.

When he finished, Richard asked him to explain what the continuing relevance of the JFK assassination was.

"Kennedy was probably the only — and certainly the last — President to ever directly condemn secret societies and the behind-the-scenes power they wield over governments and institutions," Terry stated categorically.

"Essentially, he was trying to go up against the most powerful and evil individuals in the world. I believe it is the same secret societies and the same individuals — and now their posterity — who are behind the so-called Great Reset. We're talking about the same psychopaths who are now trying to make money programmable and bring in a social credit score system under the guise of fighting climate change and dealing with pandemics. If Americans back in the 1960s had seen through the fake narrative about Lee Harvey Oswald being the lone assassin and had realised that by killing their President, the deep state had essentially nullified democracy and taken over their government, then perhaps we would never have seen 9/11 or the dozens of other false flag attacks that have killed tens of thousands of innocent people in recent decades. The whole plandemic and the global vaccination programme may never have happened."

There was a brief moment of silence in the studio as he finished talking. He looked at his watch and was surprised to see that he had spoken non-stop for almost an hour. Richard thanked him and made a final brief statement before ending the recording.

Afterwards, during a late lunch, Terry asked whether he had done okay. Both Richard and Derek—who had done many interviews—assured him he had performed well, especially given that it was his first-ever recorded interview. Over coffee, Richard revealed to them that he had been informed by a reliable source that the families of the victims of a bombing that had taken place in a northern city in England a few years earlier were planning to sue him for damages because of a documentary he had made. In the documentary, he had shown how the bombing could not have been real and how the victims were crisis actors. The aim, he said, was to bankrupt him and stop his work.

"They're going to try to do an Alex Jones on you," Derek said, referring to the lawsuits against the American talk show host in 2022 that had later bankrupted him.

"Very possibly. I won't pretend I'm not worried. My work and my channel mean everything to me, but luckily I have a large group of supporters who have reached out to me offering help if it comes to it. If they do sue me, it's going to cost me a packet, so I may have to mortgage my house to pay for my defence."

"If they do go ahead with it, and hopefully they won't, you could try launching a GoFundMe campaign or something like that," Derek suggested. "I'm sure a large proportion of your followers would gladly send you some money. Your channel is easily one of the best sources of information on false flags and fake terrorist events. Try it."

"I might have to, yes," Richard said. "Obviously I'll do everything I can to continue my work and save my channel, but losing it is still preferable to being *disappeared*... We're all just a phone call away from being rubbed out." He turned towards Terry. "You know, it was your cousin who pushed me to create my own channel and make documentary-style videos on my investigations. I remember him telling me to *always* go too far, because that's where I'd find the truth. He was a real inspiration to me."

"Thanks for saying that," Terry said, genuinely touched by Richard's words. "I didn't know it was Carl who encouraged you to set up the channel. He was quite the visionary. He must have known you'd turn it into one of the most important platforms for disseminating the truth."

"Yes, I suppose so. He had so much charisma, so persuading people to do things was quite an easy task for him. He always knew what to say and how to back it up."

"That's because he knew so much. He was a wealth of knowledge. When we were young, we'd talk for hours and hours about history, politics and current affairs. He knew so much about everything."

"I can vouch for that," said Derek. "It was Carl who first opened my eyes to the world of symbology and how everything the cabal does is forewarned about in code and symbols."

"Yes, he was an expert on that," Terry said. "You remember how every time there'd be a fake terrorist attack, he'd point out the telltale signs left behind, like pairs of shoes neatly placed next to the victims, or the number 33 appearing all the time?"

Richard nodded. "He had an eye for those things." He cleared his throat and raised his glass. "To Carl."

"To Carl."

Terry left Monmouth around five in the afternoon and headed back to Somerset. During the journey, he kept thinking about what Richard had said about them being potentially just a phone call away from being 'disappeared'. He pondered on what such an outcome for him would mean for Emily and Ollie, and whether they would be adequately taken care of. Even though he and Emily owned two properties, the barn house wasn't worth much, and their flat in Islington still had a mortgage on it. In addition, both properties had depreciated in value following the severe decline in the housing market the previous year, and their savings had all but disappeared. He knew that at some point he would have to start earning a decent income again.

He arrived back near Cudworth just before 7pm. As he was driving towards the barn house, he saw a fenced-off area a few hundred yards away that wasn't there when he had left in the morning. He drove up to it and got out of the car to investigate. On the ground inside the area were aluminium panels and steel poles which he instantly recognised as the equipment used for 5G cell masts. He walked to the side and looked at the sign that had been fixed onto the fence. It read:

NOTICE – STAY BACK!
RADIO-FREQUENCY ENERGY MAY
EXCEED EXPOSURE LIMITS

He stood there, rigid with anger. Who the hell had given permission for this abomination to appear in the pristine countryside of south Somerset, he raged to himself. *He* certainly hadn't, and he was the closest resident to it. He realised that the moment he and Emily had long dreaded had finally come. They and Ollie would now be exposed to the harmful electromagnetic frequency radiation emitted by such towers twenty-four hours a day. He turned back towards the car, head lowered but not cowed.

Chapter Three

Terry opened the door to the barn house and saw Ollie playing on the rug in front of the fireplace. Emily was on the computer looking for ideas for a wedding dress for Alan's upcoming wedding. "Hiya," she uttered as he came inside.

"Have you seen what's being installed on the hill just to the west of here?" Terry asked, somewhat abruptly.

Emily turned round and removed her glasses. "I saw some builders offloading fencing equipment earlier in the day, but then Ollie and I came inside, and we haven't been out again. Are they fencing off some private land or something?"

Terry took off his shoes and sat on the rug next to Ollie, who was building a wall with small wooden blocks. He gave him a kiss on his forehead and pulled Shylock to one side to prevent him from knocking over the rising structure.

"Do you remember what our criteria were when we started looking for a house in Somerset? Being far away from cell towers so that we wouldn't be exposed to constant radiation. That was one of the main ones, right? Well, it's not going to be possible anymore. The hill just across from here is going to be the site of a massive 5G cell mast."

Emily listened in shocked silence and dropped her face. After a few seconds, she looked up and turned towards Ollie. "So, that's it... He's going to be exposed round the clock now, after being safe from it all this time. Are you absolutely sure that's what they're installing?"

Terry nodded sullenly. "I even saw the warning sign in the fence."

"We can't accept this, Terry!" Emily railed. "We must protest to the Council or to the Police. We must do something."

"You know it won't make any difference. How many masts have been taken down because of locals protesting? Practically none. They've installed them right opposite schools and hospitals, for goodness' sake. If they could get away with that, what chance is there we'll succeed in having one removed from here, in the middle of nowhere? I'm actually surprised it took them this long to do it."

"I'll show them all the research that proves how dangerous it is, especially to children. There's so much evidence to show it harms people. Why have cancer rates shot up since they switched on the system? And besides, what on earth is 5G needed for out here? Hardly anybody lives in this area. Phone reception is okay. Who's it for?"

"You know as well as I do it's got nothing to do with phone reception or faster internet and everything to do with mass surveillance and information gathering. It's being installed everywhere on the planet, from the outer reaches of the Amazon to the deserts of Arabia. It looks like rural Somerset isn't remote enough to be left alone…"

Emily looked at him sternly. Even though she knew he was right, she was determined to call the Council the next morning to demand the removal of the installations. The following day, she called the Council to enquire whether planning permission had been granted for the erection of a huge mast in such a rural part of the county and why they—as the party most immediately affected—had not been consulted. She was told bluntly that permission was not required because of a general planning permission granted by parliament. When she raised the issue of the potential health impact on her and her family, the person on the other end casually read out what sounded like a prepared statement to the effect that there was no evidence of any risks to people's health from such installations, and then promptly hung up.

*

Over the next few days, Terry and Emily watched as the building crew installed the radio transmitters and the all-too-familiar rectangular panels on the mast, one of which was pointed directly at their barn house. At the base, they set up a supply unit to house the controls for the antennas. In addition, Terry and Emily were shocked to see four security cameras placed around the perimeter of the site to ensure that anybody trying to enter the fenced-off area or throw flammable materials towards the mast would be seen. Over the previous two years, dozens of 5G cell towers across the country had been burnt to the ground or otherwise destroyed, and most installations outside towns and cities now had CCTV cameras installed as a preventative measure.

In the evening, while they were having dinner, Terry brought up the subject again.

"Presumably we're going to start having brain fog issues again, not to mention the constant feeling of grogginess," he said.

"Alan suggested we get some shungite crystals, both to wear and to have around the house. Apparently they help reduce the effects of EMF radiation."

Terry nodded indifferently. He wasn't particularly knowledgeable about crystals and doubted whether they had the powers of protection and healing that many attributed to them.

"Okay. I suppose it can't do any harm."

"I'll go down to Yeovil tomorrow and buy some," said Emily. "There's a shop on the high street that sells them. I can't bear to think about the exposure Ollie will now be getting. He's been shielded from it ever since his birth. Now there's an antenna pointed straight at us that's emitting God-knows-how-much radiation…"

They both remained silent for a moment, lost in thought. "I keep thinking this is a sign or some sort of message for us," Emily said eventually.

"In what way?"

"Moving from London to Cudworth was undoubtedly the right thing to do in 2023, and I'm glad we did it. After what happened to Carl, I was extremely worried about your safety, as well as mine and Ollie's, so I was all in favour of escaping from it all. And living off-grid in these beautiful, healthy surroundings has been a real privilege. I've loved every minute of it, but I think there are other things to consider as well now."

"Go on."

"Ollie's going to need his own space at some point, and I don't think he should sleep in the living room. Also, next year we'll be sending him to a nursery, and the only good one I've found is a 40-minute drive away."

"Gosh, it seems like it was yesterday we were celebrating his first birthday," Terry remarked.

"Then there's the issue of our worsening finances, which we were talking about a few weeks ago."

"I know you're worried about that. It's on my mind too. Constantly."

"When you first told me about your idea of us buying a place in the countryside and bringing up Ollie in a clean and safe environment, I was all for it. But I haven't worked in almost two years now. We don't have much money coming in, and our savings are almost entirely gone. I don't want us to start penny-pinching."

Terry had written and published two books the previous year, both of which had sold fairly well initially, but in the ocean of new books that were published in the UK every year, they had inevitably been drowned out, and the royalties he was receiving were not much more than a trickle.

Emily laid out her thoughts. "I'm worried, Terry, I really am. I think we should look at all the options. If we're going to be exposed to 5G anyway, then is the case for staying here really that strong?

The rental lease for our flat runs out soon. Let's talk to the tenants and see if they'll be moving out. If they will be, let's move back to Islington for a while; I can go back to work part-time and you can focus on your bartering platform idea. I really think it's got potential. We'd keep this place, of course, and we could still spend holidays and weekends here. Then, say in a couple of years or so, we could sell the flat and find another place in the country, even more remote this time. But at least in the meantime, I'd be working and you'd have the chance to launch your business idea. You're never going to be able to do that here."

Terry was listening attentively, trying to absorb everything Emily was saying. "You've given me a lot to think about, darling." He didn't tell her he had been having the very same thoughts himself in recent days; given that *he* had been the initiator of the move out of London, he hadn't wanted to be the initiator of a possible return. "You do realise that London has become a 15-minute city, don't you?" he said after a while. "You know what that means."

"Yes, I do, but people are allowed to move out of their zones a hundred times a year at present without any restrictions. That should allow me to work twice a week without any problems. And if you do launch your bartering idea, well, it'll be mostly an online venture, won't it? Hopefully you won't need to go anywhere far too often. Plus your mother will be nearby to help with Ollie."

Terry turned towards Ollie, who was sitting in his high chair next to them. He pondered on what such a move would entail. Emily had made some good arguments, he conceded. He agreed that it did make sense to return to London, especially now that a giant mast would be blasting them nonstop with harmful electromagnetic frequencies. "When do you envisage us making such a move?" he asked her.

"By the end of summer maybe? Hopefully our flat will be vacant by then, and besides, we've got Alan's and Tracey's wedding in July."

"Okay, let's think about it. Maybe you're right."

*

Things happened surprisingly quickly over the next few weeks. Their tenants in Islington announced they would not be renewing the lease on the apartment, and Emily's former employer immediately offered her a part-time position at the veterinary practice as soon as he found out she would be returning to London, telling her he would be glad for the extra help. Another person who was pleased with the news was Ruth, Terry's mother, who had been dealing with depression ever since the sudden passing of her husband from pancreatic cancer just days before Ollie was born. Emily's parents, however, were ruffled by the news, fearing it meant they would see their grandson very seldom in future.

Upon making their decision, Terry began exploring the potential of his business idea in earnest. He came up with the name barterrealm.uk for the platform and spoke with an old friend of his who lived in Hackney and was an expert in web design to see whether he would be interested in joining him in the venture. To his relief, the friend was more than enthusiastic, and Terry now felt more confident about the whole idea.

As Alan kept reminding him, cash was gradually being squeezed out of the UK economy, and therefore he believed that the timing for such a platform was ideal. Anecdotal evidence showed that millions of people across the country were vociferously against the phasing out of cash and would happily engage with platforms or businesses that allowed transactions in ways that were not traceable or programmable. In addition, the seemingly never-ending recession had devastated household incomes and pushed millions more into financial precarity. An easy-to-use and cheap platform facilitating direct and confidential bartering would certainly resonate with them, Terry was convinced.

The highlight of the summer was Alan's and Tracey's wedding. Terry had felt deeply honoured when Alan asked him to be his best man, especially since Emily was the maid of honour. At the celebratory dinner, Tracey made a hilarious speech about how Alan had burnt the first meal he had ever prepared for her, while a slightly nervous Alan reciprocated with a funny story of his own. Towards late evening, Emily's father pulled Terry to one side.

"You'll be returning to the monster's lair soon," he said in his characteristic West Country accent. "I can't say I agree with your decision, but it is what it is. Make sure you always have plenty of food in your pantry, Terry. A huge food crisis is coming, I tell you, and we'll be seeing not just empty shelves but empty supermarkets as well. Those scoundrels in Westminster are ruining farming and sickening our animals, and the people of these historic isles are going to have a rude awakening very soon."

"Don't worry, Bruce," Terry responded, "Emily and I plan to stock up on dry foods as soon as we settle in. And we'll be visiting regularly. This move isn't permanent. Nothing is permanent any more. We'll see how things pan out and decide accordingly, but the days of certainty about the future are long gone, so we all have to play it by ear now, don't we?"

"Yes, my boy, we do. The future is looking perilous for us all, and it's our fault for not stopping these scoundrels sooner. We abdicated our responsibilities as citizens. We should have held them to account years ago."

"I wish it was as simple as that, Bruce, but halting this descent into modern-day serfdom requires a lot more than just stopping politicians from ruining us. It needs so much more, but the problem is that so many people *still* can't see what's happening, as unbelievable as that sounds. After everything that's been done to them over the last five years, they still can't see it. I sometimes feel we're living in a state of suspended reality, as if we're going to wake up from it all at some point."

"There's no magical waking up from this nightmare, Terry. We've got to tackle it head-on. This phase won't last forever. The big battle is yet to come. It'll either be us or them who decide the future."

"Yes, you're right about that. There can't really be a compromise here. It's an all-or-nothing situation. Anyway, thanks for the advice, Bruce."

"One last thing, Terry. Give young Oliver a brother or sister, for Pete's sake. What are you waiting for?"

Terry chuckled. "All in good time."

Chapter Four

Terry hadn't been back to London since his father's funeral, more than a year and a half earlier. One major change he noticed in the city was the number of two-lane roads that had been made into single-lane ones, with wide bicycle paths meandering alongside them. While the cycling paths appeared to be mostly underused, Terry noticed that the changes had made car congestion problems significantly worse. Overall, however, the city had changed little, but Terry felt that the atmosphere had a portentous heaviness about it. People seemed more compliant and less expressive — traits that neither he nor Emily found remotely appealing.

Their flat had been left in a reasonably good condition by their tenants, but it did need some freshening up, so Terry spent their first week back repainting the walls and preparing Ollie's bedroom, which had to be furnished from scratch.

Emily, meanwhile, was busy unpacking clothes and other items and buying new kitchenware. She and Terry also had to study the zoning system that had been imposed on the city in order to learn which streets marked the boundary of their zone and where the so-called 'essential amenities' were located.

Earlier in the year, the UK government had announced that following the successful implementation of pilot schemes in towns like Oxford, Leeds and Canterbury, the 15-minute-city project would now be introduced in London as well.

The official justification for these schemes was that by ensuring that all vital goods and services a person needed were within a 15-minute walk or bicycle ride from home, the need for commuting would be reduced and therefore people's carbon footprint would be minimised. The authorities had presented 15-minute communities as a utopian vision of local living, with each neighbourhood containing the range of services and facilities deemed as essential, and they had introduced the new rules with so much spin that most Londoners had simply gone along with it, or at best, had shrugged their shoulders in quiet resignation.

On the first Sunday after their return, Terry was returning to their building after a morning walk with Shylock when he saw an older-looking man sitting on the stairs outside the entrance, his elbows on his knees and his eyes shut.

As he came up to him, Terry stopped and looked down. "Hello. Are you alright? Are you locked out?"

The man, who looked to be in his mid-seventies and was wearing thick-rimmed glasses, opened his eyes unhurriedly and smiled at him. "No, nothing like that," he muttered in a deep, raspy voice. "Just enjoying the sun. My flat faces west, you see. In the mornings, I can only bask in the sunshine down here."

Terry smiled back. The man's face conveyed resilience and a strange exoticism, as if each groove of his furrowed forehead hid a unique tale of adventure and misfortune. Terry was curiously drawn to it, and he didn't want to walk past without introducing himself. "Terry Scott," he said, extending his hand.

The old man grabbed the black handrail and slowly stood up. "Conrad," he said in a firm voice as he shook Terry's hand. Shylock sniffed the man's navy-coloured leather shoes, which were spotless.

"Have you been living here long?" Terry enquired.

"Around six months."

"We've just moved back — my wife and I, and our little boy. We left two years ago to live in the country for a while."

"Oh really? Where exactly?"

"Somerset."

"Very lovely. You'd both had enough of the propagandemic, had you?" Conrad said slyly.

"That's an interesting term, Mr. Conrad," Terry grinned. "I tend to call it the plandemic or the scamdemic."

"Yes, a scamdemic is precisely what it was, young man, but the worst aspect of it all was the unrelenting propaganda. That's why I refer to it as the propagandemic."

"I agree," said Terry, pleased he now had a neighbour who shared his views on this most crucial of issues. "Do you live alone?"

"Yes, it's just me."

"I'm sure Emily would like to meet you too, and I'd love to chat with you some more. If you're not doing anything this evening, would you like to come over to our apartment and join us for dinner? Around seven?"

"Thank you very much, I'd like that," replied Conrad courteously.

"It's a bit messy still, so I hope you won't mind."

"Not at all."

"Great, see you later. We're on the third floor. Flat 303."

Terry opened the heavy framed door to the building and went upstairs. Emily was busy preparing lunch. He told her about his encounter with Conrad and that he had invited him to supper so that she could meet him as well. Emily was slightly annoyed at the short notice but was assuaged when Terry offered to prepare the meal himself.

At seven o'clock sharp, their doorbell rang and there stood Conrad, looking dapper in a navy blue blazer jacket with a silk scarf folded neatly around his neck inside the collar of a cream-coloured button-down shirt. He exuded sophistication and refinement, which Terry found charming, even if there was something of the relic about him.

Terry welcomed his guest inside and introduced him to Emily. Shylock ran over to investigate but Terry shooed him off. Conrad sat down at the edge of the sofa and called Shylock to lie next to his feet, which to Terry's and Emily's surprise, he promptly did.

While Emily and Conrad made some polite conversation, Terry studied their guest more closely. His face was well-proportioned but rugged, with a straight chin that had a large dimple in the middle. His bushy white eyebrows matched his temples, while his slightly curly pepper-and-salt hair was slicked back in a style that suggested a bygone age. There was a weightiness and seriousness about his countenance that seemed strangely at odds with his complaisant and unpretentious demeanour. Terry didn't quite know what to make of him.

"Terry tells me you've been living here for around six months, Mr. Conrad", Emily said.

"Please call me Conrad. Yes, I only moved back to England at the start of the year. I've spent most of my life abroad, you see."

"That explains your exotic accent," Terry noted with a smile. He was forever scrutinising people's accents and endeavouring to trace them to a particular location.

"Have you lived in many different countries?" Emily enquired, putting Ollie down on the carpet next to some toys.

"Yes, quite a few actually; from the Middle East to North America, I've lived in extreme heat and in bitter cold. But in case you're wondering, I'm originally from Norfolk."

"Do you have any family in the UK?" Emily asked.

"No, but I have a son who lives in Canada. I was an only child, so I don't have any siblings or nephews, nieces. My life revolves around my books now."

Terry jumped in and told him all about Barricade Books and how he had been a bookseller for almost ten years. Conrad's eyes lit up as he listened to Terry describe the kind of books he used to sell, in particular those dealing with Western esotericism and stoicism. He turned to look at the small corner bookshelf that was wedged behind the bar separating the kitchen from the living room.

"I see you've read *The Kybalion*," he said, revealing a keen sense of observation.

"Several times, in fact," Terry responded. "I suppose you have too?"

"I have indeed. I've read plenty of books on hermetic and stoic philosophy, such as the writings of Marcus Aurelius, Seneca, and so on. But the book I read most now is the Bible."

"It's nice to know that some people still read it. I imagine in times like these, there's a lot of comfort and guidance to be found in Scripture."

"It was always important to know the Bible, Terry, but you're correct — with everything that's going on in the world right now, it's more important than ever. I confess I was an atheist for most of my life, but the things I've seen in the last five years have compelled me to turn to Scripture. The dark hand of Satan has descended upon the Earth once more. Everything we're currently witnessing was written about ages ago, and the only light that can guide us through this darkness is the Bible. *Behold, I send you forth as sheep in the midst of wolves. Be ye therefore wise as serpents and harmless as doves. Be strong in the Lord and in the strength of his might.*"

Conrad's animated allocution, delivered with a gruff but stirring voice, conjured up images of a charismatic preacher rousing his audience to rapture. Terry was amused but also intrigued. "Judging from the comment you made downstairs this morning, I can tell you've seen through the monumental lies of the last few years and have understood what the real agenda behind everything is."

"I believe so, but I also believe that no single individual can fully understand what's going on. Even the cleverest can only understand a portion of the evil that has descended on the world. Some people get one aspect of it but can't see the other ones, while others see those other aspects but can't see what's right in front of them. The entire picture is quite simply unfathomable."

Terry nodded in agreement. "When do you think this assault on humanity really began? In 2019, when the 'propagandemic'—as you called it—started? Or with 9/11 and the so-called war on terror? Or perhaps even further back, with the assassination of John F. Kennedy?"

"I trace it all the way back to Ancient Babylon."

Terry and Emily waited for him to elucidate further, but he stayed silent. After a few seconds, however, he began to explain his mind.

"You see, the creatures doing all this have no ethnicity, no nationality and no allegiances except to the religion of Babylon, which they follow in a way we couldn't begin to understand. They have always sought to undermine humanity through deception. But during periods of spiritual development and human progress, this was harder for them to do, and their efforts were suppressed. But as humanity has degenerated, they have gained in strength, and as they have done so, the moral decay has become deeper, thus accelerating the degeneration. This is why human society—especially in the West—is so dysfunctional right now, so decadent, so vile. It's trapped in a cycle of degradation, which in turn feeds these parasites, who then create even better conditions for the degradation, and so it goes on. And it will continue to go on until something breaks the cycle."

Terry was impressed by Conrad's eloquence and articulateness, which he considered a fast-disappearing skill.

"Their affiliation is to their bloodlines," Conrad continued, "which have remained fairly unadulterated since ancient times. Every few generations or so, they change their surnames to hide their lineage, but essentially it's the same bloodlines that have been perpetuated through the ages. These people do not have normal human emotions. What we call conscience is alien to them. Whether they are wired differently than us or aren't in command of their senses because they worship Satan is open to debate."

"What term would you use to refer to them — to these creatures, as you call them?" Terry asked.

"You can call them anything you want, but I think it's essentially irrelevant in so far as it distracts us from truly understanding the most important aspect of all this — how they actually operate."

Even though she was engrossed in the conversation, Emily noticed Ollie yawning heavily and excused herself to put him to sleep. Meanwhile, Terry poured Conrad another glass of wine. He was tempted to reveal how he and his family had personally encountered agents of the cabal, but decided not to. He didn't want to recall the individuals who had destroyed Carl and threatened Emily and his unborn child.

"We came to some similar conclusions a couple of years back," he uttered instead. "We too realised that this group of psychopaths adhere to certain codes of conduct, such as the requirement to always forewarn us of their plans."

"That's correct. They must always inform their victims of what they plan to do. But it goes beyond that, you see. They not only forewarn you, their aim is to get you to unwittingly do the evil deeds for them. Through deception, they make parents voluntarily take their children to get injected with poison. So it's not *them* forcibly poisoning the children, it's the children's own parents doing it without realising it. The same with technology. They put awe-inspiring technology out there and people rush to use it without realising it's enslaving them."

"I agree," Terry said. "It's people's compliance that has enabled these damned psychopaths to tighten the noose around everyone's necks. With mass non-compliance, none of this would have happened. These 15-minute cities wouldn't have happened. They could never have imposed their agenda if they had come up against mass non-compliance."

"Yes, well done. But you see, these creatures know human nature better than anyone. They've studied it for thousands of years. They know what methods to use to deceive, divide and cajole. They know what percentage of the population will believe anything they're told, and what percentage will resist. They know who is susceptible to manipulation. Most importantly, they know the power of fear."

"And what is their ultimate goal, do you think?"

"The utter enslavement of the human species, of course. You see, the oldest profession in the world is not prostitution, it's slavery. And it's the most profitable. They will not stop until they have achieved the total enslavement of whoever is left after the great cull."

"That's an interesting phrase — great cull. I suppose the miscreants doing this do see us as animals that need culling every now and then. What's the term they like using? Useless eaters?"

"Yes, exactly that," Conrad said solemnly, "and the cull is proceeding at a terrifying pace. You wouldn't know it if you watched the propaganda on TV, but what we're witnessing is a genocide, or to be more precise, a democide, since it's not limited to any one ethnicity or group. And they'll use a variety of hoaxes to put the survivors into corrals. The biggest one is climate change, of course. The very notion that humans can affect the climate is ridiculous. It's obscene. It reflects how important and all-powerful we think we are. We're nothing more than ants on this giant planet, and yet they'll have you believe that our activities are changing the climate. Our activities certainly *pollute* the planet, but they don't change the climate. The climate has been changing by itself for millions of years. That's been proven, and the fact that all our activities now have to be 'carbon-neutral' shows how committed they are to depopulation. All living organisms on this planet are carbon-based. If you reduce the amount of carbon in the atmosphere, you actually make it *harder* for life to exist, which is precisely what they want. When the temperature of the planet rises, as it's doing now, the amount of carbon in the atmosphere goes up. An increase in carbon doesn't *cause* global warming, it follows it, as a natural process. They know this, which is why they're desperately trying to reduce carbon levels. Everything they tell you about climate change is the exact opposite of the truth."

As he was finishing his last sentence, Emily returned to the living room and they all moved to the small dining table in front of the balcony. While Terry served the food, Emily turned to Conrad.

"It's a breath of fresh air to talk with someone who understands what's really going on. How come you know so much about all this, Conrad?"

Conrad smiled blithely. "Just observation and deduction," he quipped. "This is first and foremost a test for every human being alive on the planet. How will we react to this demonic attempt to destroy our freedoms and alter what God himself crafted? Will we willingly accept the mark of the beast? How will we resist? Will we break this downward spiral of ever-increasing degeneration? We have done so in the past but at great cost, and this is the worst attack ever, because these Satan-worshippers now have tools they never had before. The Bible has shown me that only by returning to the bosom of our creator can we be saved. Only through God's grace can we redeem ourselves."

All through dinner, Terry listened to Conrad's ruminations with a combination of interest and amused curiosity. He was amazed at his wealth of knowledge and depth of discernment. Four years earlier, he and Emily had almost despaired at the naivety and lack of understanding that most of their neighbours had shown at the outset of the mass vaccination programme, and had refrained from discussing the issue with them for fear of causing offence. The appearance of someone like Conrad in his building was completely unexpected, and he relished the prospect of engaging in lengthy and stimulating conversations with him.

At around 10pm, Conrad thanked his hosts for inviting him to dinner and stood up, ready to leave. Upon his departure, Emily looked at Terry and grinned.

"Quite a character! He's got a face that could stop a clock."

Terry laughed. "Yes, it does have something of a timeless quality about it, doesn't it?"

"I'm sure you're well pleased now that you have a kindred spirit in the building to pour out your heart to!"

"Oh yes."

"Just don't spend too many hours chatting away with him. He might get all religious and try to recruit you."

Chapter Five

The following weeks flew by. Emily resumed her work as a vet on a part-time basis, going to the clinic in Bloomsbury on Mondays and Thursdays while Terry's mother looked after Ollie. Her former colleagues were glad to see her again, and they soon filled her in about all the latest developments and changes that had been instituted during the previous two years. Emily was shocked to find out that most inoculations which previously were administered just once were now being given to pets annually. When she asked how the animals were coping with so many boosters in their system, a colleague casually admitted that some of them didn't make it. In the two years she and Terry had spent in rural Somerset, she had deliberately shielded herself from all the awful news about mass deaths of animals across the country. Hearing this latest bit of information, she recalled how she had had to treat dozens of dogs suffering from severe liver damage when she last worked at the veterinary practice, and how disgusted she had been at the way in which the relevant oversight body had conveniently looked the other way when vets up and down the country had reported the phenomenon.

Terry, meanwhile, was busy working on his bartering platform idea. He and Martin, his web designer friend, typically spent four to five hours a day working on the website design and the platform's content management system, with Martin's spare bedroom in his flat in Hackney effectively becoming their makeshift office. Funding the venture was proving difficult, but they were doing their best to get a fully functional platform ready to pitch to potential investors.

Towards the end of September, Terry arranged to meet a marketing agency at their offices near Holborn tube station to discuss a possible collaboration. He had left the zone that included Islington only once before since returning to London, and as his car slowly crossed the dotted lines on the asphalt indicating the end of the zone, he watched as the security cameras on both sides of the road followed his vehicle, recording not just the numberplates but also its occupant. He uttered an expletive as he passed the final speed bump. Yet another conspiracy theory that's become conspiracy fact, he thought to himself.

When his meeting with the marketing company had finished, he decided to walk up to Bloomsbury to see what had become of his old bookshop. The last he had heard, it had been turned into a café, but he wanted to check it out for himself. He covered the short walk briskly, and less than ten minutes later he was standing outside the building that had housed Barricade Books for more than eight years, his erstwhile haven and the place where he and Emily had first met.

After looking at the façade for a minute, he ventured towards the door. As he went in, he immediately noticed the oppressive lighting, which he felt gave the place an intrusive and clinical atmosphere. He remembered the warmth and ambiance Barricade Books exuded, a feature his customers would always compliment him about. He turned towards the counter and looked at the offerings. In addition to the usual sandwiches, one shelf was proudly displaying a range of insect-based delicacies. Terry squirmed as he looked at the 'crunchy critters', mealworm pie and crackers with fried crickets.

A plump girl behind the counter came up to him, smiling broadly. "Hiya. What can I get you?"

Terry looked up. "Have you been selling insect foods for long?" he asked, trying to hide his disgust.

"We started this range around a year ago," she answered. "It's not for everyone, of course, but some of our customers love them. Insect protein is very good for you, did you know that?"

"Oh really?" Terry said, feigning interest. "I should try one of these, then. But not today. I'll just have a latte to take with me. Thanks."

As she was making his coffee, Terry turned around and saw two armchairs placed in the same position inside the window as when he was operating his bookshop. A middle-aged couple was sitting in them having a conversation. As he stood there, he got vivid flashbacks of Carl walking in through the door after being released from the holding facility in the Midlands, a beaming smile on his face. He recalled how his cousin had sat down in the armchair near the wall and recounted details of his detention and release. He remembered how he had brought him a glass of water, and how distraught Carl had been upon finding out about Mia's involvement in his abduction. He was so consumed with his thoughts that he didn't realise he was staring at the man sitting in the armchair, who had perceived it and was staring back at him sternly. Nor did he hear the barista call out that his latte was ready. Only when the man in the armchair pointed at her did he snap out of his cataleptic state and turn towards the counter.

"Your latte is ready, sir!"

Terry took out a ten-pound note to pay for it.

"Sorry, sir, but we don't accept cash. It says so on the door, see?"

Terry looked blankly at the sign on the door. After a few seconds, he took out a debit card and paid for his order; then, without saying anything, he pushed open the door and stepped outside. As he walked towards his car, he regretted his decision to go there.

*

Later that day, Samantha came round to see them and to play with Ollie. Due to the nature of her job as a school and couples counsellor, her work allowed her little time for escape, and she had seen Emily and Terry just twice over the previous two years, both times at Margaret's cottage in Bibury. Even though she and Emily spoke regularly on the phone, it wasn't the same as sitting down and chatting face-to-face. Now that Terry and Emily were back in London, she was looking forward to seeing them on a more regular basis.

Over tea and cakes, she began telling Emily about the new man in her life — a schoolteacher who apparently had an infectious sense of humour, despite the stereotypical assumptions made about geography teachers.

"He's lovely, Em, he really is. He's a barrel of laughs. I can't wait for you to meet him."

"We can't wait either," said Emily chirpily. "I'm so pleased you're seeing someone again, Sam. You've been alone for far too long."

"I know, and guess what; his name is Samuel, but everyone calls him Sam!"

"That's a good starting point," Emily responded. "I suppose...!"

"If he won't bore us with descriptions of scree and other geological formations, then I'll be happy to meet him," Terry said mischievously.

"He'll have you in stitches, Terry. I guarantee it."

"You must bring him round then. Let's arrange something for next month."

"Great, thanks. I'll check with him and get back." Sam took some toy bricks and started assembling them with Ollie. As she was doing so, Emily noticed an abrupt change in her. In a flash, her exhilaration was replaced with enervating sadness.

"I know Carl would like him too," she muttered, almost incomprehensively. "I can just see them laughing away over a gin & tonic." Her eyes became visibly teary, and Emily squeezed her hand in a gesture of empathy. "I'm sure he would, Sam, and might still."

"The fact that we have no body, no grave and no death certificate makes it impossible to move on. It's an open wound that just can't heal."

Emily nodded in quiet sympathy.

"How's Margaret coping?" Terry asked softly.

"She won't talk about it. Every time something happens that reminds us of Carl, she simply changes the subject and moves on. You know mum — ever the stoic... She's keeping herself busy. It's her coping mechanism. She has given herself a new assignment now. She's helping vaccine-injured people get compensation from the government. The amount is well over £100,000 for each provable case, so it can really make a difference for someone who can't work anymore because of a debilitating condition."

"That's so very noble of her," Emily said. "I admire her selflessness and resolve. I really do."

"I think it's her way of honouring Carl's work, but the deaths of the Barnards a couple of years ago also played a role. That was really close to home. At the end of the day, we must all do what we can."

"Absolutely," Terry said firmly, "in whatever way we can."

Sam wiped the tears from under her eyes and smiled.

"Anyway, how's work been since you returned, Em?"

Generally speaking, everything's fine, busier than ever. But there's definitely something that's affecting animals' health. When I first started out as a vet, most of the urgent cases we dealt with were injuries, such as a broken limb or an infected cut. But now we're seeing all sorts of strange things, like severe organ damage, sudden aggressive behaviour, loss of appetite, and so on. Two years ago, we kept seeing cases of liver damage, if you remember. Now it's broader than that — it's other organs as well."

"What do you think is causing it?"

"Well, I'd really like to know whether pet-food manufacturers have added anything new to their products. I can't help but think the problem stems from that. But there's another even more immediate danger facing these animals — the new directives requiring us to give pets all sorts of inoculations annually, even though they don't need them. I've already seen two cats die within 24 hours of receiving a totally unnecessary booster jab. And then there are these ridiculous new 'cancer vaccines'. I told my boss we're just injuring the animals, but he simply shrugged and told me we had to comply with the new rules."

Sam raised her eyebrows in genuine surprise. She hadn't heard of the new directives. "What do you think is the real purpose behind the rules?"

"I think it's scaremongering; you know, making people think that their pets are diseased and potentially dangerous unless they're given jab after jab after jab. But clearly the goal is also to reduce the number of pets—and animals in general—in the country. I truly believe that. That's why these excessive vaccinations are happening to farm animals as well."

"I read about that," Sam said. "It's the easiest way to poison our food supply even further, isn't it? I mean, whatever they inject into those poor animals will inevitably end up inside us as well, right?"

Emily nodded. "They started giving mRNA vaccines to pigs and cows last year. God knows what else they're giving them now. Poor creatures... And now they're after our pets too. It breaks my heart to see them injected so needlessly like this."

"Can't you personally opt out of giving these injections?" asked Sam.

"I'd probably lose my job if I requested something like that, but there was no way I was going to give any pets unnecessary or dangerous jabs, so I'm faking it."

"What do you mean?"

"It's surprisingly easy, actually. I just pretend I'm injecting the animal with the vaccine, but I hold a cloth underneath the syringe to catch the liquid and I distract the owner with some chitchat while I'm doing it. The fur helps conceal the fact that the syringe hasn't pierced the skin, and the animals certainly don't complain."

"Em, that's brilliant. Well done."

"I laughed when she first told me," Terry said heartily. "It's so simple. I hope hundreds of vets up and down the country are doing the same."

"Yes, so do I," Sam responded with a grin. "On a related subject, what do you think of all the delicious synthetic meats that our supermarket shelves are now full of? Isn't it delightful?"

"Delightful indeed," Emily replied, appreciating Sam's sarcasm. "I was so shocked when I first saw it. Where's all the real meat gone? All you see now is row after row of lab-grown meat, all packaged beautifully, of course, and marketed in the most glowing terms. This is one of the biggest challenges we're going to be facing now we're back — finding decent, healthy food to eat. In Somerset, we never went to supermarkets. All our food came from local farmers or our own garden."

"If only I could live like that," Sam said wishfully. "Growing our own food is going to be the only way to avoid eating all this artificial rubbish in the future. If you noticed, the few real meats still on sale are now displayed separately, like a luxury item, whereas the main section sells what is essentially lab-produced gunk. But sadly, you see most people buying it. They love it, and it's so cheap, of course."

"Is it even possible to talk about *real* meats anymore," Terry said, "given that they're vaccinating animals left, right and centre with God-knows-what?"

"Good question," Sam responded.

"This is the globalists' plan for a one-world diet," Terry continued. "Get rid of all healthy options and force everyone to eat the same ultraprocessed rubbish. Imagine how easily they can deliver toxins to the population when everybody's food comes from a small handful of global mega-corporations. Add whatever you want to it, and whoosh, instantly billions of people are consuming it without even knowing. They could be adding ground-up human waste, for all we know."

"It doesn't bear thinking about," said Sam with a look of disgust on her face. "I'd rather eat insects than fake meat grown in a Petri dish."

"I saw a wide selection of insect-based sandwiches and pies in my old shop this morning. It's become a café now. Can't say I was tempted to try any, though."

"While we're on the subject of food," said Emily, smiling, "why don't you stay for dinner?"

"Thank you, but I think I've lost my appetite! Besides, I'm meeting Samuel later for a drink." Sam got up to leave. She gave Ollie a hearty kiss and hugged Emily and Terry. "I'm so happy you're back in London. It's been quite lonely at times."

"We're glad to be back too, Sam," Emily responded, somewhat disingenuously. Even though they were making the best of being back in the city, part of her was already yearning for a return to Somerset.

Chapter Six

A few days later, Terry arranged a follow-up meeting with the marketing agency. The design for the bartering platform was proceeding well, and he wanted to discuss with the agency how they could help him pitch it to potential investors.

When the meeting was over, he began walking down Kingsway towards Aldwych. Within a few minutes, the main building of his alma mater, the London School of Economics, came into view on his left. He remembered how as a student there in the late 1990s, he would walk down the same street almost every day on his way to class, occasionally stopping for breakfast at one of the many cafes that dotted the area. The three years he had spent at university had been amongst the best of his life, and he felt a deep nostalgia not just for the carefree nature of those years but also for the more predictable state of affairs that existed in the world at the time. He recalled Mr. Johnson, his cranky and eccentric International Relations tutor who had gifted him an old Word Processor for him to use to type up his essays. He wondered what had become of him, and—if he was still alive—what his views would be on the breakdown in diplomatic relations between Russia and the West.

As he neared the end of Kingsway, he turned to look at the cars coming down the street with a view to crossing over to the other side. As he did so, he caught a glimpse of a face that was familiar. He stopped to look more carefully. There on the opposite side of Kingsway, around 40 yards further up, was Carl's best friend, Aram. He looked dishevelled and appeared to be preparing to cross the street towards his side. Even though he was visibly stockier and significantly greyer than Terry remembered him, he recognised him instantly. He shouted out Aram's name, but his voice was drowned out by the noisy traffic. He decided to wait and catch him on his side of the street.

He started walking back up Kingsway to meet Aram, who had stepped onto the road despite the heavy traffic and appeared to be looking at someone on Terry's side of the street. Terry looked at the man, who was wearing a baseball cap and dark sunglasses and was indicating something to Aram with his hand. Suddenly, Terry heard an engine rev up, and a split second later, he saw a vehicle strike Aram with full force, sending him flying over the windshield and the top of the car. Terry stood still in a state of shock. He stared at Aram's contorted body lying in the street. All the sounds around him seemed to disappear, and he watched as the cars in both lanes slowly stopped, except for the vehicle that had hit Aram, which sped off. He saw a middle-aged woman on the opposite side of the street point to it and shout repeatedly what he assumed was 'STOP'. He felt unable to move. Finally, he pulled himself together and rushed over to Aram. A small crowd had gathered around him, and as he got nearer, he saw that Aram was still breathing, even though his eyes were shut. A man was kneeling next to him injecting him with something.

"Hey, what are you doing?" Terry shouted. "What are you injecting him with?"

The man turned his head and looked at him menacingly. "I'm a doctor. Stay back."

"What did you just inject him with?"

"It'll stabilise him until the ambulance gets here," responded the man without looking up.

Terry stared down at Aram and noticed blood seeping from his mouth. He looked back at where the man in the baseball cap had been standing but he couldn't see him. Just then, he heard the sirens of an ambulance, and within seconds he was shooed away by the crew, who swiftly brought out a stretcher and—without trying to communicate with Aram or check whether he was responsive—lifted him onto it and placed the stretcher into the ambulance.

"Wait, where are you taking him?" Terry asked one of them, a burly man with a shaven head.

"To A&E, obviously," the man answered, not even bothering to look at Terry.

"Which one?" Terry didn't get a reply, so he shouted out again. "Which one?"

The man turned towards Terry in an aggressive manner, his nostrils flaring. "Why are you asking, mate? Do you know him?"

Terry's gut told him not to reveal that he knew Aram. "No, no. I was just asking."

The man stared at him for a moment, as if assessing him, then climbed inside the ambulance and shut the doors. Almost instantly, the ambulance sped off, leaving Terry and a few bystanders standing on the pavement. Terry looked around to find the man who had claimed to be a doctor, but he couldn't see him. The woman who had shouted at the vehicle that had struck Aram came up to him.

"My goodness, I've never seen a hit-and-run before. That was absolutely horrific. I'm sure the car's numberplate has been captured on CCTV. They're all over the place." She pointed a finger to one pointing in their direction from the building behind them. "It was lucky the ambulance came so quickly," she continued.

"Sorry, what did you say?" Terry asked the woman.

"I said, it was lucky the ambulance came so quickly."

Terry thought about that fact for a moment. Ambulances do not appear *that* quickly in London. This one arrived less than a minute after the accident. Surely it couldn't have been called out so quickly. His mind was racing. Just then the chaotic sounds of a busy London street came roaring back, as if someone had put the volume up again. He waited for the police to arrive but nobody did. A potentially fatal hit-and-run had just occurred, and yet there was an eerie sense of normality and regularity around him. The cars that had stopped to see what had happened just moments earlier had driven off, and traffic was flowing normally. Most of the witnesses appeared to have walked off, and the two suspicious individuals he had spotted—the man in the baseball cap and the supposed doctor—were nowhere to be seen.

"Look, I need to go now," the woman said. "I have to be somewhere. Will you wait till the police arrive and tell them what happened?"

Terry nodded, still in a daze, and watched as the woman rushed off. He suddenly realised he was the only one of the witnesses still there. He pulled his mobile phone out and called Emily. "I've just witnessed a horrific hit-and-run," he said, his voice quavering.

"What?" Emily said, startled by the news. "Are you alright?"

"I was walking down Kingsway and all of a sudden this car accelerated and hit someone."

"And then it drove off?"

"Yes. But I haven't told you the worst part."

Emily stayed silent, dreading what would come next.

"It was Aram."

"Aram? But wasn't he deported from the country? Isn't he in Egypt?"

"That's what I thought too," Terry said. "But it was him. I have no doubt. I saw him up close."

"Oh my goodness," Emily said softly. "How badly is he hurt?"

"I don't know. An ambulance came and took him."

"Did he see you?"

"No, I don't think so," Terry replied.

"Have you spoken with Sam? Does *she* know he's back in England?"

"No, but you're right, I should call her. Okay, I'll speak with you later, darling." Terry hung up and dialled Sam's number. Sam was on her lunch break and replied immediately. He told her what had just happened. She was shocked. After a moment, she told him she was not aware that Aram had returned to the UK.

"What's strange is that the whole thing looked meticulously organised," Terry said. "Aram was looking at someone in a baseball cap across the street who seemed to be telling him something, like with sign language. He was walking towards him when he was hit. And then, out of the blue, this other man appeared next to him in the street and injected him with something. I asked what he was doing but he just said he was a doctor and that he was stabilising him, whatever the hell that means. Then, within seconds, an ambulance came and took Aram away. The whole thing happened too quickly, too methodically, if you know what I mean. There was something totally abnormal about it."

"Christ, it sounds like it was a planned hit-and-run, Terry," Sam said fearfully. "Did you speak with anyone after the accident?"

"Just with a woman who also witnessed it, but she's gone now."

"Are the police there?"

"No. There's nobody here. The whole thing feels surreal, but I can see blood on the asphalt, so I know it really did happen."

"Terry, don't wait for the police. Don't be seen there. If this *was* planned, you don't want to be associated with it in any way. Go home, quickly." Terry realised Sam was right. "Okay. I'm going. I'll go back to the flat and call you from there."

Chapter Seven

Terry drove back to Islington as quickly as he could. His mind was a whirlpool of conflicting thoughts about the nature and reasons behind Aram's return to England. He had spoken with Aram several times following Carl's second abduction, and not once had he indicated that his attempts to overturn the revocation of his UK citizenship were about to bear fruit. But even if a positive decision had come through unexpectedly, why hadn't he informed him or Sam about it, Terry wondered. Why come back to the UK and keep it a secret?

He was consumed with these thoughts as he arrived home. He rushed upstairs and found Emily in the living room. She stood up and gave him a hug as he approached her.

"Are you sure you're alright?" she asked him.

"Yes, I'm fine, just a bit rattled. Where's Ollie? Is he sleeping?"

Emily nodded. "I've made lunch. Are you hungry?"

"Thanks, but no. I can't eat anything right now. But you go ahead and eat."

"No, I'll wait a bit too," Emily said. "Poor Aram. He's badly injured, isn't he?"

Terry took a deep breath and sat down. Just then he got a text message from Sam saying she was about to have a counselling session and would come over as soon as she had finished. He texted 'Okay' and put the phone down.

"Darling, there was something terribly abnormal about the whole thing. I don't think the hit-and-run was an accident."

"What do you mean?" Emily responded, raising her eyebrows.

Terry told her everything he had seen just before and during the incident, and how Aram had been taken away by an ambulance crew far more quickly than was logically possible.

"There's no way a doctor who just happened to be walking along and witnessed an accident would immediately take out a syringe and inject someone lying severely injured in the street, without waiting for an ambulance first. And who was the man gesturing to Aram from across the street? Why did *he* disappear after the accident?"

"Would you recognise either of them if you saw them again?"

"Not the man in the cap, but the doctor—if he even *was* a doctor—yes, I think I would."

"Do you really think it was a set-up?"

"I can't be certain. I don't know about the accident itself, but what happened immediately afterwards definitely gave the impression of being planned."

"If you're right, it means Aram was deliberately targeted. My goodness, Terry, they took out Carl, now they're after *him*... Are *we* next?" Emily's face betrayed a deep sense of alarm which Terry noticed instantly.

"Of course not, darling," he said reassuringly, realising he was inadvertently causing her to panic.

"Let's not stretch things too far."

"I don't want to start living in fear again, Terry. I can't do that."

"There's no need to fear anything or anybody, okay? We're above that." Terry reached for her hand and gave it a tight squeeze. "I need to go lie down for a bit. I'm feeling slightly overwrought." He excused himself and went to the bedroom to quieten his mind and collect his thoughts. Around three hours later, Sam came over and Emily let her in. She was making them some tea when Terry joined them.

"Hi, Sam. I'm glad you came."

"Hiya. Are you okay?"

"Yes, I'm fine, thanks."

"Emily was just telling me you'd be able to identify the so-called doctor if you saw him again."

"Straight to the point, I see," Terry remarked with a grin. "Maybe, yes. What I don't understand is why Aram didn't tell us he was back in England. Sam, when was the last time you spoke with him?"

"It was at least three months ago. What about you?"

"Even longer. Maybe six months. Did he say anything to you about possibly being given permission to return?"

"No, nothing at all. The only thing he said just before hanging up was that he'd avenge Carl's death. I thought it was just his emotions talking, you know, given how close the two of them were. I also remember reminding him that we didn't have Carl's body, so talking about his death was inappropriate."

"And what did he say to that?"

"Nothing. He was silent, then he said goodbye."

"What if he found a way to come back," Emily suggested, "and didn't want us to know about it because he was planning to do something drastic or dangerous and didn't want us to stop him? Or maybe he kept it secret to protect us."

"It's plausible, I suppose," responded Sam.

"Let me call his number and see if anybody picks up," Terry said, reaching for his phone.

"You mean his Egyptian number?" Sam asked.

Terry nodded as he dialled. After a few seconds, he hung up. "It's a recording in Arabic. I've no idea what it's saying."

"Terry, you must be very careful," Sam said bluntly. "We have no idea what Aram was mixed up in. He may, for all we know, have been involved in something dodgy or illegal and the hit-and-run was the result of a deal gone bad. It could all be down to something like that."

Emily agreed. "We have no clue what's going on. Hopefully, Aram will recover and contact you or Sam."

"Let's hope so," said Terry, unconvinced. He didn't believe for a minute that Aram was mixed up in any illegal activities, but he kept that to himself. He knew Aram as being squeaky clean when it came to his business transactions. No, this had nothing to do with a deal going sour; he was sure of that.

*

Two days went by without any information about Aram. To his utter surprise, not a single mainstream news outlet reported the hit-and-run, and it was only on a couple of obscure online media sites that he found any mention of it at all. They both had no more than a small paragraph on it, and both stated that the police were still looking for the driver of the car that had struck the victim.

On Sam's advice, Terry didn't call any of the hospitals in London to ask about a hit-and-run victim being brought in. He did, however, call Aram's number numerous times to see if anybody would answer, but he heard the same recording in Arabic every time. Even though he knew a couple of Aram's other acquaintances in London, he didn't have their contact details. Then, he remembered that the bishop of the local diocese to which Aram belonged was a close friend of Aram's family, so he searched online and found an office number. He assumed that if Aram was indeed being followed, any such surveillance would not extend to the local primate. He called the office. A secretary answered, and Terry asked to speak with Bishop Manoug. A few seconds later, he heard the bishop's familiar croaky voice.

"Hello Bishop Manoug," Terry said, unsure how to begin. "You may remember me. Terry Scott. I'm Carl Palmer's cousin and a friend of Aram's. Aram Saryan. I met you once a few years ago at a christening."

After a short silence, the bishop responded. "Yes, yes. I remember. How are you, Terry."

"I'm fine, thank you. I was just calling to ask whether you have any information about Aram and whether he's …"

"Such a tragedy," the bishop interrupted him. "And so young. We were all very sad to hear of his passing. May God bless his soul."

Terry was aghast. "Aram has died?" he muttered, after a few seconds.

"Yes, my son. The hospital contacted us yesterday to inform me. He was in a terrible accident and died on the spot, they said."

Terry couldn't speak. He had seen Aram alive and breathing just after the accident. He had not died instantly. Why would the hospital claim that? Eventually, he cleared his throat and asked the bishop whether he knew that Aram had returned to the UK.

"No. That's why we were all so shocked."

"Has his mother been informed?"

"Yes, I called her myself yesterday, but she has terminal cancer and is too weak to travel. She is heartbroken, of course."

"Yes, she must be," Terry mumbled.

"We will be burying him here, at Gunnersbury Cemetery, on Saturday at noon, next to his father."

"Weren't his father's remains transferred to Egypt? I remember Aram telling me he was working on that."

"He tried, but it was a complicated process, and he wasn't in the country to arrange it, so after a while, he gave up."

"Okay, thank you very much." Terry hung up and sat back on the sofa. He let the information he had just received sink in. Aram had clearly been killed in a well-organised operation, which included an operative posing as a doctor to administer what was probably a lethal dose of something, an ambulance on hand to quickly clear up the scene, and an operative across the street monitoring the whole thing. The fact that he had witnessed the event was obviously not part of the plan, and he was glad he hadn't lingered at the scene long.

But why had Aram been targeted like this, he wondered. Had he really come back to England to seek vengeance for what had been done to Carl? And how had he even returned to the country? He needed answers to these questions, if only to understand what was going on and be able to take measures to protect his family and himself. He realised there was only one way he would get those answers. He would have to go to the funeral and see who would be there.

Chapter Eight

On the morning of the Saturday, Terry told Emily he was going out for a while, and to his relief she didn't enquire where. He knew that if he told her about going to Aram's funeral, she would try to stop him. So would Sam. He recalled how two and a half years earlier, he had again taken the initiative and gone to the analyst meeting with Chimera Pharmaceuticals without telling either of them. It's the same situation now, he told himself. This is something I need to do, alone.

He set off on time so as not to be late. The cemetery was outside their zone, so he had to go past the surveillance cameras again. As he approached the road bumps, he saw a long queue of vehicles. As he inched forward towards the bottleneck, he thought of the implications that would arise if the government ever succeeded in forcing everyone to drive only electric smart cars. Not only would they have to face the constant danger of the vehicle spontaneously combusting, they would also be in a situation where their cars could be programmed to switch off if they tried to go somewhere that was deemed off limits. He had always hated electric cars, and was horrified by how their batteries could catch fire in an instant, turning the vehicle into a raging fire ball. He had decided he would rather be without a car than be forced to drive an electric vehicle of any kind.

It took him almost twenty minutes to get out of the Islington zone, and although he drove quite fast, he arrived at Gunnersbury Cemetery slightly late, at ten minutes past noon. As he walked through the massive gates, he looked for a crowd of mourners but he couldn't see anyone. He walked further in. Eventually he saw a gleaming black hearse parked a short distance to the right of the main pathway and a small group of people standing in a rough circle. He was too far to recognise anyone. He began walking towards them stealthily, trying to make as little sound as possible and using the large trees scattered around the cemetery as cover. As he got closer, he caught a glimpse of one of Aram's friends whom he had met at a party years earlier. In all, he counted just nine people, amongst them Bishop Manoug, who was conducting a graveside service, and four pallbearers.

He was about to go forward to join the mourners when he caught sight of a man in a black suit standing under an oak tree around thirty yards behind the bishop. He gasped as he realised he recognised the man. It was Raul. The same Raul who had worked and conspired with Mia. The same Raul who had threatened him, Emily and their unborn child. The same Raul who—for all he knew—was behind Carl's twin abductions and untimely demise.

Terry felt his heart beating frenziedly in his chest and he broke into a cold sweat. He immediately turned around and walked hurriedly back towards the gates. As he exited the cemetery, he ran to his car and drove off, swerving sharply as he turned onto the main road. What the hell is going on, he hollered to himself. Was Raul responsible for Aram's death? Was he at the cemetery to see who would attend? Was Aram secretly working for the cabal? He felt the veins in his temples pulsate as the memory of his previous encounter with Raul came racing back. He took a deep breath and tried to stay calm.

When he arrived back home, he saw Conrad sitting on the steps of the building.

"Hello, Terry. How are you?"

Terry sat down next to him, feeling he needed a breather before going upstairs.

"Are you alright?" Conrad asked him. "You look distracted."

"I've just been to the funeral of a friend who was killed in an accident a few days ago."

"Oh, I see. So sorry to hear that. I assume he was a young man, like yourself?"

Terry nodded as he stared blankly into the distance. Neither of them spoke for a while.

"You think you know someone," Terry muttered finally, "and then, in an instant, you realise that what you thought you knew was just an illusion."

"People are complex creatures, Terry, and the world we live in is more complex than you could ever imagine. There's an ocean of chaos out there, and only few people know how to navigate it."

"How does one even *begin* to learn how to navigate that ocean?"

"It begins with an awakening, and that awakening happens when a man realises he's going nowhere and doesn't know where to go."

Terry exhaled heavily. "That's exactly how I feel right now. I thought I'd undergone a deep awakening a few years ago when the plandemic began, but now I'm not so sure. I thought I was discerning when it came to people, but maybe I'm not."

"Not everything is as it seems," Conrad continued, "and don't expect to be able to understand everything. Even the most knowledgeable of people don't understand everything that's going on. Some get it more than others, but nobody can see the whole picture. This world isn't designed so that humans can understand everything. Remember, there's no other species on earth with such extremes of intelligence and stupidity as humans. There are the pathetic little humans who disappoint and shock you with their shallowness, and then there are the extremely enlightened ones who amaze you with their perceptiveness, and a million shades of stupidity and intelligence in between."

"What about the deceivers who mask their true identities, who are the opposite of what they say they are?"

"The deceivers, you say; there are lots of them in the world, too many to count. But once your awakening reaches a point of no return, you start seeing them for what they are. You learn how to unmask them. That's why it's so important to surround yourself with the right people who can guide you towards the truth. It speeds up the awakening process."

Terry was instantly reminded of Carl's reference—exactly three years earlier—to a 'tribe of the awakened' comprising people of all shades and backgrounds. "I'm trying," he said eventually, "but avoiding the deceivers or the shallow people, as you call them, inevitably means not engaging fully with society, and that's not good either, is it?"

"Correct, it's not good. But avoiding those people doesn't mean you cannot engage with them. Do so with aloofness. Treat reality like an illusion. We can never know everything about it anyway. Be above it all, and when some people get too much for you, just shake them off or take a break from them. There's nothing wrong with that."

"Reality *is* an illusion, yes," Terry responded, rising to his feet. "I think that's something we've all learned in the last few years — that nothing is what it seems. Right, I need to go upstairs to talk with Emily about something, but thanks for imparting more of your wisdom, Conrad."

Conrad grinned. "What you call wisdom, Terry, is merely knowledge acquired at great cost."

Terry patted him on his shoulder and hurried upstairs. He found Emily sitting by the computer. "Darling, I want to talk to you about something. About where I was this morning."

Emily swivelled her chair around. "Okay, I'm listening."

"I went to Aram's funeral."

"Oh my goodness, he died?"

"Unfortunately yes."

"How did you find out?"

"Do you remember Bishop Manoug? We attended a christening once where Aram was the godfather and we had a chat with him. He had an extremely hoarse voice."

"Yes, I remember."

"I called him, and before I could tell him why I'd called, he blurted out that the hospital had informed him about Aram's death and that the funeral was on Saturday."

"Terry, why did you keep this from me?"

"I'm sorry for doing that, but I simply *had* to go to the funeral and I knew you'd try to talk me out of it."

Emily bit her lips agitatedly. Even though she was annoyed by his furtiveness, she knew he was right. She would most certainly have tried to prevent him from going.

"As I expected," Terry continued, "there were hardly any people there, since nobody seems to have known he had returned to England. Even the bishop didn't know."

"Was his mother there?"

"No. Apparently she's got terminal cancer and can't travel."

"Did you find out anything about the hit-and-run?"

"I didn't go up to the mourners."

"Why?"

"I don't know how to put this, but there was someone there I recognised."

"Who?" Emily asked, bracing herself.

Terry took a deep breath. "Raul."

"What?" Emily cried out. "And Mia too?"

"No, just him," Terry said.

"Did he see you?"

"I don't know. He may have."

Emily rubbed her temples nervously. "Terry, is it all starting again? Are we going to be sucked into another nightmare?"

"No, definitely not. It's..." As he was talking, the doorbell rang. Terry looked in the direction of the front door. "Are you expecting someone?" he asked.

"No."

Terry went to the door and looked through the peephole. What he saw jolted him like an electric shock. He stumbled back. It was Raul.

Chapter Nine

Emily guessed who it was just from the look on Terry's face, which had gone eerily white. She jumped up from the sofa but stood rigidly still, not knowing what to do. She felt a shiver go down her spine.

Terry looked through the peephole again. Raul seemed to be alone, but he couldn't be sure of it. What if there's a trained killer standing just out of sight, he thought, his adrenaline rising. Would Raul even need a killer to do the job?

"What the hell do you want?" he shouted from behind the door.

"Open the door, Terry. We need to talk."

"What about?" Terry asked nervously.

Emily rushed towards him. "Unless you leave right now, I'm calling the police," she yelled in a panicky voice.

"You're not in danger. If we wanted you dead, you'd be dead already."

Terry pulled Emily away from the door and whispered to her to go to Ollie's bedroom and lock the door. "If you hear any commotion, call the police."

Emily grabbed her phone and rushed to Ollie's bedroom. Terry waited until she had locked the bedroom door, then slowly opened the front door, leaning against it in case Raul tried to force his way in. He peered through the gap apprehensively. Raul was standing a couple of feet away from the door, his jacket off and arms outstretched to the sides. A sinister smile accentuated the offensiveness of his already minacious gaze, and the disconcerting amber of his eyes had a piercing and disorienting effect on Terry.

"See? I'm not armed," he gibed, patting himself down to indicate he wasn't carrying a gun.

Terry came out into the hallway.

"No, not here. Inside."

Terry got a vivid flashback of the first time he saw those emotionless crocodile-like eyes, and recalled the revulsion he had felt at having to listen to an operative of the cabal talk so casually and matter-of-factly about Carl's abduction. After a few seconds, he regained his grip and stepped back inside the apartment, pointing to the large yellow armchair in the far corner of the living room. "Okay, I'm listening," he said, staying on his feet.

Raul walked over to the armchair and sprawled across it. "Sit down, Terry," he snarled.

Terry moved slowly towards the dining table and pulled out a chair.

"You've got an annoying habit of turning up in places you shouldn't be at," Raul hissed. Terry stayed silent, maintaining a watchful glare.

"Why did you go to the funeral?" Raul enquired.

"To try to find out more about Aram's death."

"And are you any wiser now?"

"Look, I know it wasn't an accident. I saw the hit-and-run."

"I know you did."

"So it *was* you in the baseball cap."

Raul looked at him impassively.

"What I don't understand is, why go to such lengths to organise an elaborate hit-and-run?" Terry said. "Why not do it quietly, out of sight, like you did with Carl?"

"We had our reasons. Besides, Aram was a very wily type, a typical Levantine. He had a craftiness about him that was interesting, to say the least. Plus he had money. Getting a new passport from another country to re-enter the UK was a direct challenge to us. It had to be dealt with."

"What was he doing here?"

"Poking his nose into things that are our domain. Clearly his expulsion from the UK and the disappearance of his friend weren't enough to make him smarten up."

"Where is Carl?" Terry demanded to know, his voice raging.

"You already know the answer to that."

"Will he be coming back at some point?"

"No. Not this time."

Terry felt an almost uncontrollable urge to leap across the room and strangle Raul. He pictured his dead body lying on the floor, his shifty eyes lifeless and still. Just then, the bedroom door opened and out came Emily, closing the door firmly behind her.

Raul glanced at her disinterestedly. Terry had hoped she wouldn't leave the bedroom, but now she had, he knew it was pointless to tell her to go back to it again.

"Come sit here," he said, pulling out the chair next to him.

Raul returned the enmity in Emily's glare. "How's the little boy doing?" he asked smugly.

"Why are you here?" Emily retorted with a steely tone in her voice. "Did you come to threaten us?"

"We don't threaten people, my dear. Why would we? I could have rubbed you out in that stupid little barn house of yours if it was required. But it's not. I just want to tell your annoying husband to keep his head down and stop turning up in places he doesn't belong in. We're in the final stage of the transformation. There isn't long to go now."

"Long to go till what?" Emily said.

"The final conclusion, of course."

"And what's that?"

"The elimination of choice." Raul's eyes glowed like fiery lanterns as he looked at them sneeringly.

"You mean the elimination of free will?" Terry almost shouted.

"No, we're not capable of doing that yet. People will still have free will, just no choices."

"People will resist what you're doing," Terry declared firmly. "They won't continue accepting sheepishly whatever you decide to dish out to them."

"We have installed the means to nullify people's capacity to resist."

"You can't control every single individual on this planet that way," Emily retorted. "You didn't succeed in getting *everyone* into your bloody AI matrix during the plandemic."

"No, but we succeeded with enough. Those who remain outside it are a thorn, but nothing more. They keep us alert, which is good, but we have plans for them."

"You mean for us," Emily snarled.

"Only if you choose to be thorns," Raul muttered, standing up and putting on his jacket. "Keep your head down, Terry. You don't want to get hurt. And watch what'll happen next week. The end game is finally here."

He walked to the front door, flung it open and exited the apartment. Terry rushed to the door and locked it. He turned around, fully expectant of Emily's wrath.

Emily moved quietly to the sofa and took a long, harrowed breath. Terry sat down next to her.

"I can't tell you how sorry I am. I couldn't have imagined he'd be at the funeral and would follow me here."

"It's not your fault you witnessed the hit-and-run," she said softly. "And why do you think he followed you? If he knew where we were living in Somerset, of course he knows where we live in London."

"Yes, I suppose you're right."

"Was it even a coincidence you happened to be there at the exact moment of the hit-and-run?"

Terry was taken aback by Emily's insinuation. He had never thought of it as anything other than pure chance that he saw Aram getting mowed down.

"Remember what you were telling me about the universal principles in *The Kybalion*?" Emily continued. "*Chance is but a name for law not recognised*, or something like that?"

Terry nodded. "Regardless, I shouldn't have gone to the funeral today. That's what drew this psycho here."

"Psycho or not, he's right. They've always known where we are, and they *can* get to us wherever and whenever they want. Perhaps things really *are* coming to a head now. Maybe they really are about to unleash everything they've got and go for it lock, stock and barrel."

Terry thought about what Emily had just said. It was true that the pre-2020 world they had known no longer existed, but some vestiges of it still remained, despite all of the dystopian measures and actions that had been taken since then. If Raul was indeed telling them the truth and the end game was about to be played out, what sort of world would they wake up to one day, he wondered.

He rubbed his eyes in troubled contemplation. "I don't know what to do. I've got to keep this beast of a creature away from us, but I feel like they're pulling me back into something I can't let us get involved in again. I mean, should I simply not leave the apartment? Should I stop communicating with people? I just don't know."

Emily held his hand reassuringly.

"Terry, you've never stopped doing what you've been doing, and I don't want you to now. Ever since Carl's disappearance, you've been active in the resistance in one way or another; you've taken part in protests outside vaccination centres, you've stopped children getting the jab — you almost got arrested the last time you did that, remember? And I've always supported you, because I know that burying our heads in the sand was never an option. Whilst doing these things may be dangerous, it's what thousands of others are also doing every day, so I'm okay with it. But you promised me one thing when Ollie was born — that you'd never talk openly about what it was that Carl remembered after his hypnotic regression. I told you then that if there was one guarantee you'd meet the same fate as Carl, it was you trying to shed light on that. As long as you keep your promise, do whatever you feel you have to do, and I'll do my bit too. We're in this struggle for Ollie's sake. There's no shirking our responsibilities."

Terry gave her a tight embrace.

"We're never going to be free from them," Emily said, almost whispering, "so we might as well continue doing what we can. I refuse to live in fear."

"You're right, darling. It's fear that's our greatest enemy, not these sadistic psychopaths."

Chapter Ten

Upon deciding to move to Somerset two years earlier, Terry and Emily had given their two TV sets to friends and had decided that in the barn house, they would spend their evenings reading books and playing with Ollie. During their time there, they had received their news mainly from alternative news channels on the internet and through platforms such as Telegram. They hadn't regretted their decision to dispense with television once, and were relieved at not having to endure the blatant propaganda and deeply slanted news coverage of the mainstream media.

Terry avidly followed a host of commentators he trusted, most of whom had been de-platformed by the social media giants. The content providers he watched ranged from doctors whose information was untainted by big pharma money to geopolitical experts who offered refreshingly original analyses of the Ukrainian war and other conflicts. He also enjoyed listening to a commentator with a roguish cockney accent whose main weapons were a highly questioning mind and a unique style of talking that was heavily peppered with colourful obscenities. He marvelled at how the most complex of theories and explanations could be made so comprehensible through the use of language that had the power to call things as they were and to entertain at the same time.

Following their return to London, he and Emily had debated whether to get a new TV set, but had eventually decided against it. They still had a sizeable collection of films on DVD they could watch on their home movie screen, and they also didn't fancy the idea of paying the BBC licence fee again. Besides, they were more than happy to continue devouring books in the evenings, and they both had a large to-be-read pile at the side of their bed.

*

An hour or so after their confrontation with Raul, Emily called Sam to tell her about the encounter and to relate what Raul had told them. Sam wasn't as shocked about his turning up at their door as Emily had expected, having already become convinced that Aram had been killed on the orders of the same individuals who had snatched Carl. Apart from admonishing Terry for going to Aram's funeral, she didn't have much to say, except to express her deep worry that they were all getting dragged into a perilous situation yet again.

Later that evening, Terry scoured the internet to see what major events were planned for the following week. Raul's allusion to something that was about to happen was ambiguous, so he didn't know what to look for precisely. A scan of the websites of the mainstream news publications revealed that the WHO would be holding a conference at its headquarters in Switzerland at which a 'panel of experts' would be discussing the hypothetical scenario of a major Ebola-like epidemic erupting in Africa and spreading rapidly to the rest of the world. He also read about a press conference that was planned for the following Wednesday at which senior figures from the IMF would be elaborating on the 'increased risk' of a major bank run in Europe, and how—if necessary—depositors' money would be used to save the banks — the infamous policy of 'bail-ins' that had first been wielded in Cyprus twelve years earlier.

Terry wondered whether it was any of *these* events that Raul had alluded to. They seemed to be very much in the vein of other meetings that had been convened since the summer by supranational bodies to warn the public about some impending financial or health-related calamity. Could the warnings this time be the harbinger of a *real* catastrophe, he thought to himself. He had never doubted that the debt-laden economies of the West would collapse at some point, and he had always believed that the trigger would be a deliberate action whose timing would not be fortuitous.

Suddenly he remembered hearing about a summit meeting that was going to be held in London on the following Friday between the Prime Minister, the CEO of Chimera Inc., and the head of the Global Economic Council, or GEC. Roughly a year earlier, Chimera Pharmaceuticals had announced that its name would be changed to reflect the fact that it no longer dealt exclusively with vaccines but was now a major global player in financial and AI products as well.

He searched for more information on the summit. According to the BBC, the trilateral meeting was being convened in order to finalise arrangements for the introduction of facial recognition in many spheres of interaction between the public and the government, as well as digital identification as a requirement for purchasing certain goods and services, including train and airline tickets and petrol.

In these roll-outs, the leading role would be played by Chimera Inc. as part of a broad partnership with the UK government. The main instigator of this partnership was apparently the GEC, whose ageing head had become a mainstay at global conferences and summits over the previous decade. Terry read a few more articles about the upcoming summit, including one by a cynical commentator who claimed that it was only a matter of time before the government required digital identification for accessing the internet. The article went even further and argued that the day was not far when people who were deemed to be too meddlesome would be barred from using the internet simply by having their digital identification disabled. The fact that such a critical article had been published by a mainstream news outlet came as a surprise to him.

Terry sat back and thought about what these schemes really meant. He found it shocking that the UK government was willing to grant a foreign company authority to track UK citizens indiscriminately and to collect detailed information about their movements and spending patterns. Surely this is an abrogation of the government's responsibilities towards the public, he thought to himself. And why on earth is an unelected body like the GEC which represents the interests of the world's billionaire class involved in facilitating such schemes between a supposedly sovereign government and private corporations?

In Terry's mind, this sort of merging of state and corporate power was the very definition of Fascism, and yet—as with everything else the government had done over the last few years—the response of most journalists was invariably to portray such developments as a positive move — in this particular case, the phrases used included 'a step towards ensuring a safer internet' and 'a blow to scammers'. Where were the mass demonstrations against this illegal intrusion into people's private lives and spending habits? Where were the tens of thousands of people who during the pandemic had come out onto the streets to protest against the government's arbitrary and nonsensical measures? Were they waiting for the day of the summit to take action? Had they given up?

Sunday morning began with thundery weather, and Terry noticed a chill in the air as he took Shylock for a walk. After a late breakfast, he went downstairs to Conrad's apartment. Conrad opened the door with his usual beaming smile and let him in.

"I hope you don't mind me popping round like this," Terry said.

"Not at all. You're always welcome."

"Do you have time for a quick chat?"

"Sure," Conrad replied, leading him into the living room. Conrad's apartment was like a time capsule from the 1970s, and it reminded Terry of the house in Haringey he had grown up in. Two armchairs with wooden armrests and antiquated upholstery stood near the balcony, and a small matching sofa with worn-out cushions sat awkwardly in the middle of the room. A 1930s radio with names of capital cities on the front panel stood on a tall table underneath an ornate mirror, and a large three-shelf book cabinet with glass doors—seemingly antique—stood against the wall. Terry moved closer to examine the collection.

In addition to Winston Churchill's *A History of the English-Speaking Peoples*, he noticed a large number of books on the two World Wars, a volume of Lord Macaulay's essays, Kahlil Gibran's *The Prophet*, and several modern editions of books on classical philosophy.

On the floor underneath the cabinet—placed there due to their weight, Terry assumed—was the full set of the 1966 *Encyclopaedia Britannica*. He bent down to admire the vintage hardcover and the gold-coloured lettering on the spines.

"You can tell a lot about a man from his book collection, can't you?" Conrad quipped.

"You certainly can. Is your Bible here too? Can I have a look at it?"

Conrad went into the bedroom and fetched a King James Bible with a badly worn leather cover. Terry opened it carefully. "Published in 1959, I see. It's fairly old, isn't it?"

"There's a reason for that. The new editions have important messages removed, did you know that?"

Terry shook his head.

"Yes. For example, many references to the power of praying and fasting have been deleted. We're now in the age of bible censorship, Terry. That's why it's important—if you want to start reading the Holy Scriptures yourself—to get hold of an older version."

"I'll keep that in mind, thanks. You've had this one since childhood, presumably."

"I have indeed," Conrad said, lowering himself into one of the armchairs by the window.

Terry placed the Bible on the coffee table and moved to the other armchair. He looked out through the balcony door at the rain that was still pouring down. He didn't mention Raul's visit to their flat the day before. Instead he brought up the subject of the upcoming summit.

"I was wondering whether you'd heard about the summit meeting the Prime Minister will be having next Friday during which he'll be announcing the roll-out of digital IDs. Before we know it, people will be required to provide their ID number before travelling or filling up their car."

"I *have* heard about it, yes. It's not all that surprising, though, is it?"

"I suppose not. We shouldn't be surprised by anything our politicians do anymore. But in a way, it brings into focus just how bad our government and our public institutions really are. I mean, wherever you turn, in whatever field, the worst people are in charge. In politics, the most corrupt and incompetent nincompoops are in the highest positions of power. In medicine, the most compromised individuals are steering or influencing policy. In academia, the country's top institutions are led by the most blinkered and dogmatic of people, and in the media, news is concocted and delivered by the most mendacious people imaginable. Up is down, right is wrong, left is right, bad is good. How the heck did we arrive at this point?"

"Terry, what you're describing is a classic kakistocracy," Conrad said with a look of seriousness Terry hadn't seen before.

Terry had never heard of the term before. "What's that?"

"It's where a country as a whole is run by the worst elements of society, and it's an absolute prerequisite for bringing about the one-world government these demonic creatures want. That's why pretty much every country in the world is a kakistocracy right now. It's taken them decades to remove people of any worth or integrity out of positions of power and replace them with bought-off or compromised individuals. You see, in order to make people accept a one-world government, the elites first need them to lose all faith in their national institutions. By turning governments into dens of corruption, abuse and incompetence, you create apathy and indignation. People will stop engaging in the political process and will feel abandoned and hopeless. Then, when the system collapses and institutions no longer function as they were meant to, they will become desperate and demand a radical solution. That's when global technocratic institutions will be presented as the only effective alternative to failed national institutions. The parasites running the show aim to crash everything, because it's the only way to create what they want. They need everything to burn down. It's the only way their phoenix can rise — out of the ashes."

"I'd never thought of it that way," Terry remarked, scratching the back of his head. "I can see the logic in it, though. I mean, it can't be a coincidence that most Western nations are now ruled by degenerate or demented clowns. And it's been like this for years. You can definitely see the apathy; most young people consider it completely pointless to vote, and everyone can see how the NHS has failed them, how their freedoms are being eroded away, and how the economy is skewed against them in favour of the giant multinationals. But when the inevitable collapse comes, will they really accept world government in its stead? I'm not so sure."

"They won't be given a choice."

"I think the process will be bloody horrible to witness," Terry said, recalling Raul's statement about the elimination of choice.

"Yes, it will be, but Providence will ensure that the phoenix that'll emerge from the ashes will be *our* phoenix, not theirs. However, first, humanity must undergo a huge cleansing. We have become rotten to the core, and only after a mass purgation, can we even think about salvation."

Terry nodded silently, not wishing the conversation to go in the direction of biblical canons and prophesies.

"Conrad, if you don't mind my asking, what exactly was your line of work?"

Conrad seemed to be in no rush to respond. "I was in the intelligence-gathering business," he muttered eventually. "Private, not state. That's why I've lived most of my life abroad."

"What sort of intelligence did you gather?"

"All sorts. From secret company documents for rivals to military secrets for governments, we did it all."

"Interesting…" Terry remarked, wanting to know more but sensing that Conrad didn't want to divulge any more information.

"It's only now," Conrad continued unexpectedly, "in my twilight years, that I'm able to make amends for the lives we shattered. To give something back." He slowly turned his head towards the balcony window next to him and with his stubby finger began tracing a rain drop as it zigzagged down the glass. His eyes narrowed as he appeared to recall something distressing.

"We were motivated solely by the huge fees and cared little about what harm we were causing by trading in such information. If only I'd known back then that everything has a cost, every effect has a cause, as it says in that book of yours."

"You mean *The Kybalion*?"

"Yes. You can't run from your sins forever. They'll always catch up with you, if not in this life, then definitely in the next." Conrad sat perfectly still in his armchair, his eyes shut but eyelids twitching slightly.

Terry felt he had outstayed his welcome and got up to leave. "Thank you, as always, for your insights, Conrad. It's so refreshing to hear your take on everything. Stay seated. I'll make my way out. Take care."

As he walked up the stairs to the third floor, he pondered on what Conrad had said about governments being deliberately set up to fail in order to pave the way for a one-world government. It certainly rang true. The same disastrous policies being implemented concurrently across the globe did certainly imply a central hand behind it all. But didn't that also imply that a strike at the very centre would release the prey—in this case, all of humanity—from the tentacles that were drawing it ever closer to oblivion? He didn't believe for a minute that changing a single government here or there would stop the slide towards catastrophe, but what about a strike at the *nexus* controlling all the world's governments? That could change the game entirely. He was sure of that. He reached the front door to his apartment. He could hear Emily and Ollie playing inside. He put on his usual smile and went inside.

Chapter Eleven

During the course of the following week, Terry tried to focus on the task of preparing a formal marketing plan for barterrealm.uk. Together with Martin, he began adding some flesh to the pointers he had shown to the marketing agency at their last meeting so that work on a proper pitch could begin. But at the back of his mind was the series of events that were scheduled for the days ahead. His gut was telling him that something out of the ordinary would be happening at one of these events, but he didn't know what exactly, or indeed at which.

As the week progressed and the conferences at the WHO and the IMF came and went without incident, he wondered whether he had been wrong in his assumptions and whether Raul had been referring to something completely different, such as an unscheduled event or a bombshell announcement of some sort. He read the official news coverage about the two conferences and found that nothing unexpected or new had been discussed or announced. Both conferences had dwelt on the topics which newspaper articles and official communiqués had stated they would.

As Friday rolled around, he doubted whether it was even worth it to watch the live feed of the meeting at Downing Street which the main news channels would be broadcasting. He found it strange that such prominence was being given to this particular meeting, but assumed it was because of the nature of the expected announcements; perhaps the government was hoping that by giving the event so much publicity and importance, the new rules it would be announcing would affect the public's consciousness and seem like a *fait accompli*.

The weather had improved slightly that morning and Emily had gone for a walk to Highbury Fields with Ollie. Terry was sitting at his desk in front of two computers; he was using Emily's one to watch the live feed as he worked on his own laptop. Even though he had lowered the volume, he could still hear the discussion taking place as a host of political analysts were brought on to explain how Britain would be a safer and better place with the introduction of digital IDs and facial recognition.

He was still only half-listening when the reporter abruptly ended the discussion and announced that the Prime Minister was about to address the nation. A few seconds later, the Prime Minister—looking uncharacteristically weary and tense—came out of No. 10 and walked towards a large microphone a few yards in front. He was followed by the President of the GEC—who despite being over 80 looked sprightly and alert—and the CEO of Chimera Inc., who had a beaming smile on his face.

The two men stood on either side of the Prime Minister but slightly behind him, while behind them assembled a group of tall, well-built security agents, all dressed in uniform black costumes, white shirts and dark sunglasses. The two agents standing just behind the head of the GEC had very conspicuous earpieces attached to their left ears.

Terry sat back to listen to what was going to be said. The Prime Minister cleared his throat and began speaking. As he spoke, Terry got the feeling that he was reading from a script that was in front of him but out of view of the camera. The speech seemed too rigid, too punctilious to be impromptu. Its main thrust was that the UK was facing unprecedented risks in the field of cyber security, and that the spreading of fake news and misinformation had reached such levels that it was now imperative to shield ordinary citizens from the dangers posed by such activities. To that end, the government had no choice but to institute new rules whereby everyone using the internet would first have to provide verification of their identity using digital IDs. Moreover, facial recognition would be used to make people's interaction with governmental bodies speedier and more secure, and both of these major 'reforms' would be made possible due to a far-reaching collaboration between the government and Chimera Inc. The timescale for full implementation of the schemes would be six months, the Prime Minister declared, ending his speech by urging the public not to fall for the 'crazy conspiracy theories' that many individuals would inevitably spread on the internet about the government's true intentions.

Throughout the speech, cameras could be heard in the background snapping pictures, and Terry was sure he heard a scoff or two from the crowd of journalists as the Prime Minister was talking.

Upon finishing his speech, the Prime Minister stated that he now wished to hand over to the President of the GEC, who would explain in further detail the global nature of the cyber threats facing the UK. As the head of the GEC moved forward towards the microphone, there was a frenzy of camera flashes. Who the hell does he think he is, Terry thought to himself. And why are our detestable press treating him like a celebrity?

Grinning from ear to ear, the GEC President prepared to speak. In a thick Austrian accent, he thanked his host for the opportunity to address the British people and explain how what he called the 'Fourth Industrial Revolution' would affect their lives. Just then, a shot rang out and part of his brain got blasted out of his head from the left temple. As he fell to the ground, the two agents with earpieces who had been standing behind him turned around and wrestled someone to the ground. Terry stared at the screen in utter disbelief. Everything seemed to be happening in slow motion. Just before the camera turned away, he caught a glimpse of the shooter, who was on the ground being immobilised. It was Raul.

There was utter pandemonium as chaos and panic erupted, and Terry could hear a crosscurrent of shouts and screams. The reporter who had been covering the event rushed away from the scene as the live feed was cut and a shocked news presenter in the broadcaster's main studio appeared on the screen.

"We are getting reports of a shooting at No. 10 Downing Street," she said, her voice unsteady. "It happened during the live press conference that the Prime Minister was giving following a summit meeting with the heads of the GEC and Chimera. Early indications are that the founder and President of the GEC has been shot and injured by an assailant, who has been arrested at the scene."

For a few seconds, the presenter seemed lost for words and appeared to be waiting for instructions on what to say next. A few moments later, the reporter at the scene appeared on the screen again, this time from somewhere on Whitehall. He was clearly struggling to compose himself.

"We have been moved away from Downing Street by the police and an ambulance has arrived at the scene. I can confirm that the injured party is the head of the GEC, and I can also confirm that the shooter was apparently a member of his own security detail."

Terry couldn't believe what he was seeing and hearing. He hadn't spotted Raul standing amongst the security agents, but he instantly knew that *this* was what he had meant in his last cryptic statement before leaving their apartment. Just then, Emily walked in with Ollie and saw Terry's ghost-white face. "Are you okay?" she asked, visibly concerned.

Terry pointed silently to the screen on the computer. Emily came over and saw the words 'Breaking News: Shooting at No. 10 Downing Street' moving from right to left at the bottom of the screen.

"My goodness, they've shot the Prime Minister?" she asked apprehensively, putting her hand across her mouth.

"No, the head of the GEC. He's dead."

Emily stood quietly for a moment, trying to take in the news. "Was it a sniper?" she asked finally.

Terry shook his head. "One of his own security people. Raul, in fact."

Emily felt her heart miss a beat. "How do you know it was him?" she shrieked.

"I saw him clearly, darling. I'm positive it was him."

Emily rushed to the sofa to sit down. "Raul's just murdered one of the most powerful men in the world and he was *here*, in our apartment, less than a week ago?"

Terry nodded quietly, his eyes heavy under the strain.

"Terry, what if someone saw him come here? They're going to think *we* were involved in this..." Her eyes became visibly teary as a feeling of dread came over her. Terry moved to the sofa and sat next to her. Shylock came up to them and sat by their legs, sensing their anxiety and dysphoria.

"Don't think along those lines," Terry said firmly. "Right now, we're clueless as to what's happening."

"What does this mean?" Emily whispered. "Raul works for them, doesn't he? He's one of them. Why has he done something like this?"

"I really don't know. I have no idea what's going on. I always assumed he worked for Chimera, but maybe there's more to it than that."

"At least we now know what he meant when he said 'Watch what will happen next week'. Clearly, this was planned well in advance."

"Yes, undoubtedly, but did he act alone? Who else was in on this? And why the GEC scoundrel? Did Chimera order this? And why in this dramatic fashion?" Terry's mind was awash with questions and theories. Just then, his phone rang. It was Martin. He too had been watching the news and was equally aghast. While he and Terry were talking, Sam tried to call too. Finding his phone engaged, she called Emily, who promptly told her that the shooter was none other than Raul.

"Oh my God, Em, what's going on? Who *is* this Raul? First he goes after Carl, then Aram, and now he does this? Is there a connection we're not aware of? I don't understand what's happening."

"Neither do we. My head feels like it's going to explode."

"Try and stay calm, Em. We can talk later. Just tell Terry I called, please."

"I will. Thanks. Let's talk later." Emily hung up and waited for Terry to do the same, which he did a few seconds later.

"We haven't asked the most pertinent question yet," she said, turning towards him.

"What's that?"

"Why did Raul forewarn us about something big happening? I mean, why tell us anything at all?"

"Maybe it was just a slip or a boast. Or maybe he was toying with us. I mean it's not like he gave the secret away. We had no clue what he meant when he said what he said."

"What if he told someone that he informed us in advance of the assassination plan?"

"Stop thinking that way, Emily," Terry said, almost shouting. "He told us nothing, okay? Nothing at all!"

Emily dried her eyes, but there was no hiding her deep apprehension as to what could happen next.

Chapter Twelve

News of the killing of the head of the GEC spread around the planet almost instantly. Within an hour, most of the world's mainstream media were reporting on nothing else, with the killer being variously referred to as 'an unknown assailant' or 'a member of security'. As the day progressed, a series of live statements were broadcast on official news channels, including by the Commissioner of the Metropolitan Police and the Prime Minister himself, both of whom expressed outrage at the assassination and stated that whoever was involved would be ruthlessly tracked down and brought to justice. Meanwhile, leaders around the world also issued heavily worded condemnations, with the US President being particularly caustic and threatening, using words such as 'reprisals' and 'payback'.

By mid-afternoon, the police had already announced a series of arrests, without, however, revealing any information about the identities of the arrestees. As he listened intently to the news broadcasts, Terry tried to rationalise what was happening. He had no doubt that the GEC was one of the principal organisations of the globalist cabal. Its prognostications read like a chronology of the events that had transpired around the world over the previous decade, and given that almost every prediction it made came true, its annual conferences invariably garnered global attention, with observers scrutinising every word uttered by the participants in order to get an indication of what the organisation's main focus over the coming year would be.

Terry had been studying its activities ever since the beginning of the pandemic. In his opinion, one of the most egregious manifestations of its tentacular reach across the globe was its coterie of young 'global leaders', all of whom had been specially trained over many years and then opportunely placed into positions of power to implement policies which the GEC had been propounding for years. The UK was no exception. These heads of government seemed to have several things in common — an expert knowledge of how to manipulate or twist reality to suit their agendas, an eerie ability to smile while talking about a horrific or tragic event, and absolute ruthlessness in dealing with protestors or anyone opposed to their policies. But the most revolting of their traits, in Terry's mind, was their sheer cowardice, manifested in their refusal to ever be questioned or interviewed by a real journalist.

As the hours passed, in addition to following the news on the mainstream news outlets, Terry kept an eye on posts and comments on alternative media channels. He had not been surprised in the least when within minutes of the assassination, many commentators on these channels had posted celebratory messages glorifying the killer and hailing the event as the beginning of the end of the globalists' power. One post read 'The head of the snake has been chopped off, the body will now wither away; freedom is near!!!'

Whilst he didn't share the optimism in such sentiments, he understood why some people were seeing the killing as a big step towards destroying the cabal's reach. Clearly, the loss of such a senior figure in its hierarchy would impact the elites negatively. However, he had also seen a few posts that warned the public about what was likely to come next, arguing that the globalists would now unleash their wrath and intensify their assault even further. One well-known poster even argued that the elites themselves may have been behind the killing as a way of justifying what they wanted to do next.

During the course of the day, Terry noticed with growing alarm how the mainstream media's tone was becoming increasingly vitriolic and malicious. In addition, one by one, global organisations were issuing condemnatory statements that seemed uncannily similar in language and content. He detected a clear message being conveyed in all of them — the already-announced plans for central bank digital currencies, the transfer of national sovereignty to supranational bodies, and the gradual elimination of cash would not be abandoned.

Furthermore, news analysts and political correspondents began talking—almost in unison—of subversive and dangerous elements in society that had to be expunged, since they were 'undermining confidence' in the work of elected governments. Terry knew exactly what sort of individuals they were referring to.

After regaining her composure following her initial shock, Emily had decided not to listen further to the news. She had instead gone to Ollie's bedroom and was keeping herself busy there. Terry was relieved, since he didn't want her to hear the almost ceaseless opprobrium and threats emanating from every mainstream channel.

Towards evening, just as they were preparing for supper, Terry and Emily heard their doorbell ring. They both jumped, but to their relief, it was Sam. "How are you two holding up?" she asked, coming inside quickly. She joined them at the kitchen table and immediately noticed how pale Emily looked.

"We're still trying to take it all in, to be honest," Emily responded, her face creased with worry.

"That's understandable. Not even in my wildest dreams could I have expected—much less hoped for—such a thing. I mean, an assassination on the steps of Downing Street..."

"And broadcast live as well for the whole world to see..." Terry noted. "There's no doubt something huge will be happening over the next few weeks. A killing like this doesn't just go away quietly."

"What do you think they'll do to him? To Raul, I mean?" Sam asked.

"It'll probably depend on whether he was part of a conspiracy or whether he acted alone," Terry replied. "If it's the former, those behind the plot may eliminate him before a trial can be held, just like they did with Lee Harvey Oswald."

"Whatever they do, I hope he suffers," Sam muttered.

"I'm sure he'll never see the light of day again, if he's even still alive. But, as beastly a miscreant as he was, it's not impossible that he had a change of heart about everything he'd done and wanted to stop this madness by striking at the head of the monster. I know it's unlikely, but who knows? What I find most intriguing is that he chose a moment that would ensure maximum visibility. I mean, he could have shot that pathetic little toad *before* the cameras turned to him, or he could have shot him away from the cameras altogether. By waiting for that exact moment, he clearly wanted the whole world to witness the killing. He definitely planned it that way, and there must have been a reason for it; something symbolic perhaps, or maybe it had something to do with their code of conduct. We know how important their stupid code of conduct is for them."

"You're right," Sam agreed. "But there's another possibility as well, one that may sound completely outlandish. What if he was being controlled remotely, like through mind control, and did the shooting without even being aware of it? I'm sure they've got the technology to control people that way. After all, they wiped Carl's memory, didn't they?"

Terry raised his eyebrows in curious fascination. "It's a hell of a frightening thought, but I suppose it's possible. However, my gut tells me he was aware of what he was doing, and the reason he did it is more prosaic. But whatever the true reason, he must have known he wouldn't get away with it."

"Do you think Mia is involved in all of this too?" Emily asked quietly. "After all, we know she and Raul were working together."

Terry was surprised he hadn't thought of that possibility. "I haven't a clue. She might be."

"For all we know, she may be amongst those who've been arrested," Sam blurted out before Terry could stop her.

"They've already started arresting people?" Emily asked nervously. "Have they said who exactly?"

Sam rushed to reassure her. "No, no, but you've got to stop worrying, Em. There's no evidence tying you two to anything."

"You know as well as I do these people can manufacture any evidence they want." Emily said, almost in a whisper. "If they want us locked up—or worse—they'll do it." A long silence ensued.

"How are the girls?" Terry asked Sam eventually, trying in vain to change the subject.

"They're okay, but they're shocked, obviously. I spoke with Lizzie on the way here. She said that a group of students at the university marched through the campus in celebration after news of the killing broke. The staff apparently tried to stop them, but the more they were told off, the larger their numbers became."

"I'm sure other universities are seeing similar things," Terry remarked. "Quietly, most of the world must be overjoyed by this. I wonder whether the assassination will embolden people to become whistleblowers and come forward. We might even see the elites' puppets break ranks." He reached for his phone to check the latest news.

"Please put it down," Emily beseeched him. "You've been staring at your phone and computer nonstop for hours. Let's just have a quiet supper without discussing this any more. Please. It's too much, it really is."

Terry put his phone down on the small corner table. "You're right, darling, sorry. Let's talk about something else." Even though Emily had said repeatedly that she refused to live in fear, he could tell she was struggling to suppress her growing anxiety.

Chapter Thirteen

The following day, Terry went downstairs to Conrad's apartment to garner his views on the previous day's dramatic events. Conrad opened the door in his vest. "Hello Terry," he said jovially. "I was expecting you."

"You were? Terry asked, surprised.

"Yes. I assume you want to discuss what happened yesterday."

"I do indeed, if you've got the time."

"Unfortunately, I'm just getting ready to go somewhere, but why don't you and Emily come down for supper this evening? With your little boy, of course. It's my turn to host."

"That's very kind of you, Conrad, but we couldn't impose on you like that."

"I insist. I'll make some pasta, it's not difficult at all."

"Okay, thank you very much! We'll bring something too."

"I'll expect you at around 7pm."

Terry returned to his apartment and informed Emily of the invite. Earlier in the week, they had made plans to go out for dinner on Saturday evening, but following the assassination and the subsequent arrests, they had changed their minds. Going to Conrad's for dinner would still be an outing, he thought, and Conrad's effervescent company would be a welcome change for Emily. To his relief, she agreed.

During the course of the morning, Terry found it hard to concentrate on anything work-related. He tried several times to go through the marketing plan he had been preparing, but he couldn't focus on the task. Around midday, he opened the BBC's main website to see what the latest news was. As expected, there were precious few details about the identity of the assassin, and absolutely no mention of possible motives. The police were refusing to divulge his real name or nationality, and their main focus appeared to be beefing up security in and around the capital. In fact, the mainstream media channels seemed to be reporting on little else other than the presence of heavily armed policemen outside government buildings and at the country's ports and airports. Even though the Prime Minister had stopped short of declaring a state of emergency, he had repeatedly urged people to avoid crowded areas and report any suspicious-looking activities to the police.

Similarly, there was very little information about the CEO of Chimera, the only news being a brief statement issued by the company the previous day condemning the killing as an 'act of global terrorism' and offering the police its full cooperation in the forthcoming investigation. The company had also stated that its CEO was safe and had already returned to the US.

Terry tried to remember what his first impressions of Raul had been when he had first encountered him at Chimera's analyst meeting. He had felt that he was not native British, and that Raul wasn't his real name. He recalled how when he had confronted Mia at the meeting, it had infuriated him that he didn't know what her real name was. Now, he felt the same frustration about not knowing Raul's real name, even though he knew it made no difference at all. He wondered how the two of them could have met. How the hell does the cabal find and recruit such people, he thought to himself. Is there a special process for applying to work for them? Are agents recruited from a young age and trained to become ruthless enforcers? Do they do whatever it is that they do purely for the money, or is it a power trip? Is blackmail involved? Terry's mind was racing with questions.

As seven o'clock approached, he helped Emily prepare a bag of toys for Ollie to play with in Conrad's apartment. "Prepare to go back in time now," he told her jokingly, recalling the strange sensation he had felt when he had first walked into Conrad's living room.

"I feel like that every time we go to your mother's," Emily said with a grin.

Conrad opened the door with his usual welcoming smile. As she entered the living room, Emily noticed the large mirror on the wall to her left. "Wow, this is beautiful!" she remarked, admiring its ornate gold-coloured frame.

"It was my parents'," Conrad explained. "Edwardian. They made everything beautifully back then." He offered them a drink and some crisps and poured himself a large whiskey.

Emily sat down on the small sofa with Ollie on her lap. Conrad came over with a glass of wine for her and poked Ollie playfully in the belly, eliciting hearty giggles.

"I was wondering," Terry said inquisitively, "would yesterday's events be the kind of thing you'd gather intelligence on if you were still doing what you used to do? Would you be tasked with collecting information on the shooter, for example?"

"Possibly, if a non-state actor wanted information they knew wouldn't be made available to the public."

"How would you go about finding such information?" Emily enquired. "If you don't mind my asking."

Conrad made himself comfortable in his favourite armchair next to the balcony window. "Not at all. We'd use one or more of our tried and tested techniques. We had a good range of them."

"Could you give a hint or two as to what these techniques were?" Emily asked puckishly.

Conrad threw her a wry glance.

"Well, sometimes we'd have to infiltrate an organisation to find out from the inside what was going on. Or we'd pay someone to divulge the information we wanted. We had many ways. People are easy to manipulate, you see."

"So you were a bit like a spy, I suppose," Emily persisted, intrigued by Conrad's past profession, which Terry had told her about.

"That sounds very James Bondish. Our work was a bit more banal than that."

"What's your assessment of what happened yesterday, Conrad" Terry asked. "How do you see things developing as a result of this killing?"

"How do *you* see things developing now?"

"Well, the authorities are clearly lashing out in anger. As far as I know, there's never been an assassination in Downing Street, not even an attempted one, so it was to be expected they'd double down on their plans and issue threats in all directions. After all, they've been humbled and humiliated, but I think it's all bluster. They have lost one of their top figures and strategists. He was without doubt one of the main planners and instigators of their depopulation and transhumanism agendas. His demise can't not weaken them, surely."

"So, what do you expect will happen next?" Conrad pushed him.

"I really don't know, to be honest. There's a massive face-off going on right now between them and the people. It doesn't really matter who the actual assassin is, or that he was one of their own. The whole world has seen that these elites are killable, they're vulnerable. And they've been shown to be complacent and arrogant. Surely this will inspire other assassins to pick off their remaining leaders. Once the top figures are eliminated one by one or go into hiding, hopefully this nightmare will come to an end."

Conrad waited for a moment before responding. "Terry, these creatures can't be defeated through violence. Sure, they've attacked humanity with demonic violence and cruelty, but we cannot end this nightmare by reciprocating in kind."

"I agree," said Emily firmly. "We cannot go to war with them in the traditional sense."

"They can only be defeated if the energy they feed on dries up. You see, these creatures feed on fear, desperation and other states of mind that create negative energy. The world is currently drowning in such energy, and has been for years. But when enough people stop living in fear and start loving others while respecting themselves, then a point will be reached when the total amount of positive force will exceed the total amount of negative force. That's when you'll see these demons wither away. They'll be raging and writhing, but nobody will hear them. They'll be giving orders but nobody will be obeying them. They will wilt and die without the need for any bullets. Only self-awareness and unconstrained love will defeat their hate, and not even Satan himself will be able to halt the process."

"You're right," Emily said. "They fear love because it creates a world they can't control." Conrad smiled at her in quiet approval.

"Why do you think the killer did what he did?" Terry enquired. "What do you think his motive could have been?"

"It could've been anything. It could've been something as simple as disaffection in the ranks. He may have felt he'd been skipped over for promotion or something like that, and took out his frustration on his boss. It's happened before. Organisations such as these present a united, monolithic front to the outside world, but they're racked with internal divisions and personal vendettas, just like any other organisation. Plus, of course, they're all psychopaths and narcissists. So, add that into the mix and it's not surprising that such a killing took place. It was certainly interesting that it was done in such dramatic fashion, for everyone to see, but I wouldn't attach too much importance to it, Terry. One killing will not stop this madness. Neither will ten. Only when a sufficient number of people wake up one morning and say ENOUGH, I refuse to comply, I refuse to be afraid, will the grip of these creatures start weakening. People need to wake up spiritually and realise what they truly are — divine creations of God whom nobody can enslave. All we can do is hope that that day isn't far off."

Terry listened to Conrad's assessment of the situation with facile fascination. It's certainly a novel perspective, he thought to himself. He sensed, however, that this form of thinking must have come to him recently, and that years ago his take on the event would have been considerably different. He assumed that his new-found interest in the Bible must have been the cause of the change.

"Isn't it a bit naïve to expect that there's going to be a mass awakening around the world and that billions of people are suddenly going to realise they've been lied to and deceived over the last five years? I mean, we both know that the crowd neither seeks nor wants knowledge."

"Not at all," Conrad averred. "I think it's naïve to think that these creatures can be 'picked off', as you termed it."

"Well, maybe not assassinated as such, but surely we should start seeing them getting arrested now. The evidence against them must be as long as my arm."

"That's not going to happen either, Terry. As much as we would all love to see them in handcuffs being paraded in front of the cameras, it's not going to happen; at least not until *after* they've been defeated. For the time being, they continue to own the judges and the police. They are untouchable, and they will remain so until the majority of people stop complying with rules designed to enslave them. Once that happens, you'll see the police change sides. But if people try to go after the elites with violence, the police will respond with violence."

Terry had long hoped for the kind of mass awakening that Conrad had just alluded to, and in the three years since Carl's first disappearance, he had done everything he could to educate both himself and those he encountered about what was going on in the world. While he *had* seen a few people awaken to the fact that not everything was as it seemed, he had been deeply disappointed by how most people had dismissed the very notion of a nefarious agenda being implemented by the globalist elites, despite all the evidence to the contrary.

"Anyway," Conrad said, returning to his usual geniality. "Let's eat, shall we? The food will get cold."

Emily put Ollie on the floor and emptied the bag she had brought with her. Ollie looked gleefully at the pile of toys in front of him and promptly began preoccupying himself.

They sat down at the small square kitchen table Conrad had prepared. An orangey glow was emanating from a ceiling lamp hanging low over the table, giving a cosy yet peculiarly interrogatory feel. Emily admired the perfect symmetry with which the cutlery had been laid.

Conrad had made tagliatelle with a creamy courgette and garlic sauce. "This is delicious, Conrad," she said, savouring the flavour. "It's al dente, just the way I like it, and not too creamy."

"You're a dab hand at cooking, I see!" Terry said, filling his mouth.

"I *had* to learn how to cook well. My wife was an excellent cook, but she and I divorced when the kids were still young, so I've lived alone most of my life."

"Oh, you have another child as well, apart from your son in Canada?" Emily asked.

Conrad looked up contemplatively, and Terry and Emily noticed an abrupt change in his demeanour. In a flash, his jovial countenance and radiance had disappeared, replaced by a precipitous malaise.

"I had a daughter as well," he muttered, "but she died recently." He gazed towards the balcony window.

"I'm so sorry, Conrad," Emily said softly. "I didn't mean to bring up painful memories. I had no idea."

Conrad took in a deep breath. "It was my fault, ultimately. Had I been a better father, she may not have strayed into the enemy's camp."

Terry and Emily didn't understand what he meant by that statement, and they didn't want to press him to explain. But they didn't have to.

"You see, I was almost always absent during their childhood, away on work. My son was a timid child, but my daughter — she was a fiery girl, and very ambitious." Conrad rubbed his furrowed forehead as he recollected old memories. "Every time I'd see her, she'd interrogate me about my travels and where I'd been, what I'd done. She wanted to follow me into the intelligence-gathering business, but I told her it was a dangerous profession and not one I wanted her to go into. Being of a rebellious character, the more I'd tell her no, the more she wanted it. Then, when she was at university, she was recruited."

"By MI5, you mean?" Terry enquired.

"No, by the enemy."

"You mean a foreign power?"

"I mean the same enemy we're facing now."

Terry stared at Conrad apprehensively. Is he referring to the cabal, he wondered. "What exactly did they recruit her for?" he asked gently.

Conrad gulped down the remaining whiskey in his glass and poured himself another glassful. "She had many talents, foreign languages being one of them. And she had a way with people. She always knew how to get what she wanted. Even though 9/11 had opened my eyes to the possibility that behind-the-scenes actors were driving the world towards an unbearable, slavish future, I still didn't know the full extent of what was to come. We in the intelligence business knew instantly, of course, that it was an inside job, but we could never have imagined the scale of the propaganda and lies that would follow, nor that those lies would lead directly to where we are now."

Terry and Emily sat in commiserative silence, waiting for Conrad to continue.

"Then, when I found out who she was working for, I tried to pull her out. I begged her to stop. That's when she cut me off completely, and I lost all contact with her. Of course, it was incredibly naïve of me to think she could ever escape that world. Once they've recruited you, you can never leave. Well, not alive."

"How did you find out she'd passed away?" Emily enquired cautiously.

"Just under a year ago, I got an anonymous letter informing me that she was dead," Conrad replied, sighing. "It said she had died in a honeytrap operation gone wrong. Strangled to death." A look of anguish came over him as his wrinkled face became mangled with grief.

"What was her name?" Terry enquired, trying to be circumspect and respectful.

"Jasmine. It was my mother's name."

"A beautiful name," Terry said.

"This is my punishment," Conrad said wretchedly, "punishment for a life led impiously, recklessly, selfishly. Getting into bed with companies like Chimera was her way of getting back at me for not having been there for her when she was growing up."

Terry felt a shiver go down his spine at hearing the name Chimera. "Did she ever use any aliases?" he blurted out without thinking.

"I assume so. In covert operations, everybody uses aliases. Why?"

"Just wondering, that's all," Terry replied quickly, his mind now racing crazily. He looked at Emily, who was sitting diagonally to his right. He could see that she was thinking the same thing he was. "Do you have any pictures of your children?" he asked. "I'd love to see some."

Conrad nodded and slowly pushed back his chair. He moved unsteadily towards the tall table under the ornate mirror and pulled open a drawer. Inside was an old-style family album. He returned to the kitchen table, sat down and opened it. When he found the picture he was looking for, he turned the album towards Terry and Emily. The photograph showed two teenagers standing in a garden — an awkward-looking boy of around sixteen with acne and unkempt hair, and a slightly younger-looking girl with braces on her teeth and a cheeky grin. Terry stared at the photo in stunned silence. From the expression on his face, Emily realised immediately that Jasmine was indeed Mia.

"Really lovely picture, Conrad," Terry said finally, trying the get rid of the lump in his throat. "Did the anonymous letter you received say anything else?"

"No, only that Jasmine's death had occurred a few months earlier and that I shouldn't expect a police investigation. Also, that I wouldn't be given her body."

"You mean you weren't even able to bury her?" Terry said, genuinely shocked.

Conrad shook his head slowly.

"Is there a chance the letter was a fake, that she isn't dead after all?"

"That was my initial hope, so I made enquiries using my old contacts. It took a while, but I eventually got confirmation from two reliable sources that it was true. She *was* killed."

Conrad lowered his face and covered with eyes with his stubby fingers, his harrowed breathing indicating deep pain.

Terry put his hand on his shoulder in empathy. "I'm sorry we made you bring all this up, Conrad. We didn't know. I apologise."

Conrad wiped his eyes and raised his head. His face was sallow and tormented. "I can only imagine how many lives she ruined too, just like I did. God forgive us both."

Terry felt he had to push the conversation towards a different direction, but his mind was blank. "Where in Canada does your son live, Conrad?" he asked eventually.

Conrad waited a bit before replying. "Halifax," he muttered, clearing his throat.

"And what does he do?"

"He works for a non-profit organisation. They help homeless people and those in extreme poverty."

"Very noble of him. Is he married? Does he have any children?"

"Not yet. He travels a lot, so he says he doesn't have time for a serious relationship. But he knows he has to give me a grandchild before I die."

"I'm sure he will." Terry noticed that Emily was looking uneasy and on edge. He quickly finished his food and gave her a nod. Emily excused herself and started collecting Ollie's toys, while he got up and took the plates to the kitchen sink.

Conrad offered them coffee but Emily politely declined, saying it was time to put Ollie to bed. She and Terry thanked him for dinner and wished him goodnight, apologising again for having brought up painful memories. In the lift on the way up to their apartment, Terry turned to her and held her hand firmly.

"We must never tell him that the assassin the whole world's talking about was his daughter's partner-in-crime. That would break him."

Emily nodded. "Do you think it's possible that Raul and Jasmine were lovers, and the reason why Raul killed the head of the GEC was because he held his bosses responsible for her death, for sending her on a dangerous mission?"

"I don't think anything's impossible anymore."

"Do you think Raul knew that Jasmine's father lived here, in the same building as us?"

"Undoubtedly. And it must have been him who sent the anonymous letter."

Chapter Fourteen

Things developed in the country far more rapidly and dramatically than even Terry could have imagined. By Monday afternoon, the government had announced a raft of new measures, including a temporary ban on demonstrations, hefty fines for anyone posting online images or footage of the assassination, and criminal prosecution for anyone praising or justifying the actions of the assassin. Immediately following the announcement of the measures, Terry saw on social media that members of the truther community—now calling themselves 'the Rebellionists'—had begun organising a massive protest in Central London for the following day, posting details about the starting point and the commencement time on Telegram and other platforms. They were calling for a peaceful defiance of the ban on demonstrations and an immediate rescinding of the new measures, which they considered an unprecedented assault on human rights and freedom of speech.

Terry decided to refrain from taking part in the protest, having promised Emily he wouldn't do anything excessively risky over the next few weeks, or at least until things had quietened down a bit. On the day of the action, he looked online for live coverage of the demonstration but found no mention of it anywhere in the mainstream media. Neither was there any mention of the demonstrations that had been planned for other cities in the country. Within an hour after the scheduled start of the protests, however, he began seeing posts on social media from participants describing some sort of attack on them. A short while later, he received a call from Martin, who—unbeknownst to him—had gone to the London demonstration and had been at its forefront as the protestors were approaching Trafalgar Square.

"Terry," he mumbled, breathing heavily. "You weren't there at the square, were you?"

"No, I didn't go. Were *you* there? Are you okay? I'm seeing talk of an attack of some kind on the protestors."

"They had some sort of directed-energy weapon. Just when we were, you know, entering Trafalgar Square, they must have switched it on. I've never felt anything so fucking horrible and painful in my life."

Terry could hear commotion in the background. "Bloody hell, are you alright? You don't sound okay. If you're feeling unwell, please go to A&E."

"No chance, mate," Martin responded, coughing. "They'll be looking for us there. I'll go home and lie down for a bit, then I'll call you." He hung up. Terry tried to suppress the sense of alarm he was feeling at hearing that directed-energy weapons had been used in the heart of London. He had heard of such weapons before but didn't know what they actually did. He went back on Telegram to see what further information he could gather on the abortive protest march. Soon, a handful of the commentators he followed appeared on the platform to report the use of a crowd-control sonic weapon that had made hundreds of demonstrators nauseous to the point of collapse. One commentator stated that he believed microwaves had also been used, and that he'd seen dozens of people with awful skin burns.

Terry wondered whether *this* was what Raul had meant when he had told him two years earlier that he hadn't seen anything yet and that when they used their best weapons and technologies, he would drop to his knees in awe. He called Emily to show her what he was seeing. Emily, who was in the bedroom, came over and was instantly shocked by the news. "Oh my God, they're microwaving people now?"

"Martin was there too. I think he's been injured. He called a few minutes ago and he sounded scared. Hundreds of demonstrators seem to have been injured in some way, through burns or radiation or I don't know what."

"Terry, what the hell is going on?" Emily cried out. "I don't recognise this country anymore."

"I'm not sure I do either."

*

In the evening, Martin called Terry from his home to talk about what he had experienced at the protest march.

"Are you okay now?" Terry asked, deeply concerned.

"The pain's largely gone, but I tell you, it was the most awful sensation I've ever had. It felt like my body was being cooked from the inside, like the water in my skin was heating up. And then there was that horrible feeling that I was going to be sick at any moment. We all just ran to get away from the square."

"So it's now official — they've started using bioweapons against people in the UK too. I remember them doing this in Australia back in 2022, during anti-government protests there. I can see why they'd do it, to be honest. I mean, why go to the trouble of deploying large numbers of policemen to do old-fashioned riot control when you can disperse crowds easily and quickly using advanced technology? Did you even see any policemen there?"

"We saw a few on the way to Trafalgar, but none in the actual square, which tells me they knew the square wasn't safe and so they stayed at a safe distance. Terry, quite a few demonstrators were writhing in pain on the ground. They couldn't walk. I don't know if they've survived. It was absolute chaos, mate. Placards were strewn across the square. It looked like a battle had taken place."

"What did the placards say?"

"Different things, like THIS IS NOT MY GOVERNMENT and DO NOT OBEY, DO NOT COMPLY, things like that."

"Were there any people you recognised there?"

"A few. That cockney guy you listen to on Telegram was there. I saw him keeled over, like he was going to be sick. Also that former Big Pharma executive who's now on our side. I spoke with him briefly before we reached the square."

"Could you see where the actual weapons were?"

"I think they were on the elevation outside the National Gallery, or that's what it looked like, at least. There were suspicious-looking men standing behind the large columns; I assume it was they who were operating the equipment."

Terry took in a deep breath. "This is bioterrorism. Our so-called government is now nothing more than an agency of globalist terrorists."

"No doubt about it, mate."

*

Over the following weeks, Terry and Emily barely left their apartment. Emily asked for a fortnight's leave from work, and Terry postponed several meetings he had arranged in Central London. Despite their lingering fears, however, no investigators or police came to their door to question them about knowing Raul. As a precaution, though, they decided to never mention the name in phone conversations or online communications with anyone, in case they had been bugged or hacked, and Sam agreed to do the same.

They also refrained from seeing Conrad. The revelation that Mia had been his daughter had come as a profound shock, and they both felt there was something deeply incongruous and questionable about the whole thing, including the circumstances in which Conrad had moved to their building. As much as he wanted to believe Conrad's account of his life and his alienation from Mia, Terry still had nagging doubts.

Even though Emily kept herself away from the news, Terry continued following developments religiously — both through the mainstream media and on alternative news platforms. In his opinion, there was far too much happening for him to be wittingly unaware of it. He noted that the assassinated head of the GEC had been replaced by his principal henchman, who—according to numerous commentators on Telegram—was an even more fanatical exponent of transhumanism than his predecessor had been.

Terry's overwhelming sense was that the timeframe for the implementation of the globalists' agenda had been brought forward due to the assassination. He based this assessment on the government's repeated announcements that the process of moving to a cashless society in the UK, where the only legal tender would be digital currency, was to be accelerated. Terry had no doubt that the globalists' end game—the yardstick by which the success or failure of their whole enterprise would be measured—was the universal introduction of programmable money. However, he detected a touch of desperation in these and many other pronouncements the government was making, noting that each new announcement was merely serving to alienate and anger the public even more.

Alongside the increasing tension and nervousness in the air, which Terry and Emily were feeling intensely, they also began experiencing a return of one of the primary symptoms of constant

5G exposure — persistent brain fog. Terry, who was more sensitive to electromagnetic frequencies than Emily, had suffered from it considerably prior to their exit from London two years earlier, and had only found respite in the rural setting of their barn house in Somerset. But now, several months into their return, the condition had returned, and he was finding himself struggling to remember or hold onto thoughts.

Around three weeks after the assassination in Downing Street, Terry called Richard Andrews to get his take on the event. They hadn't spoken since Terry's panel discussion with him and Derek Johnson in the spring.

"Richard, hi. It's been a while. How are things? Are you well?"

"Nice to hear from you, Terry. Yes, I'm fine, very busy in fact. I'm trying to find out as much as I can about the shooter so that I can produce a documentary on the assassination early next year. I don't expect the mainstream media to report anything about him, and his trial—if he's still alive—will be a closed one, so we won't find out any details about him from that either. This may be the last project I work on, so I'm in a rush to complete it."

"Why your last project? What's happened?"

"I'm being sued by the relatives of the alleged victims of that bombing I made a film about a few years back; do you remember me telling you about it?"

"Yes, I do. Damn, they've actually gone ahead with it?"

"Yep, and they're asking for several million quid in damages. The aim is to bankrupt me and close down my channel. I think they're going to succeed in doing both."

"Richard, I'm so sorry to hear that. Do you have a good lawyer fighting your case?"

"I do. He was recommended to me by one of my followers on Telegram, and he's preparing a solid defence. But as we both know, if a decision has been made somewhere high up to close me down, that's what will happen. That's why I'm in a rush to complete my investigation into this assassination."

"I can help you with that," Terry said.

"Really? How?"

"Will you be coming to London at all? I prefer to talk face-to-face."

"I understand. I'll be there in early January. We can meet up then."

"Okay. Take care, Richard. We'll talk soon."

Chapter Fifteen

As the year-end approached, Terry found himself remembering the awful Christmas three years earlier when they had all met at Margaret's cottage in the Cotswolds and spent Christmas Day together without knowing whether Carl was alive or not. He recalled the sense of emptiness and trepidation they had all felt, as well as the premonition he had had that 2023 was going to be a momentous year. Now, as 2026 approached, he realised he was having the exact same feeling.

He was glad, at least, that his mother would be with them on Christmas Day. Following her husband's death just a few days before Ollie's birth, she had spent the next two Christmases with them in Somerset, and Terry didn't want to disrupt what had effectively become a tradition.

Terry collected his mother around noon, since she no longer drove. A year earlier, she had been diagnosed with a nervous system disorder that had affected her motor skills, and she had had her driving licence withdrawn as a result. Terry considered the disorder a vaccine injury, since the initial symptoms had appeared just weeks after her first jab, but Ruth had dismissed such speculation as hogwash. He had also noticed that she seemed to be experiencing accelerated ageing, a phenomenon he had seen in many heavily vaccinated people. In contrast to Margaret, who had not taken the vaccine, she—along with Terry's father—had taken several boosters in addition to the first two shots, and while she steadfastly refused to accept any connection between the vaccines and her physical ailments, Terry himself had few doubts. He knew that if she deteriorated any further, she would have to move in with them or have a social worker come daily to help her with everyday tasks.

Emily greeted her warmly as they entered. It was a cold day, and she had left the heating on all morning to warm up the apartment. As they sipped on mulled wine, Ruth played as best she could with Ollie and, in a worried tone, asked the question Terry and Emily were expecting.

"Has anybody come round asking about that killer?" She had been in a state of interminable panic ever since the assassination of the head of the GEC, and her constant agitation—combined with her worsening depression—had conspired to affect her mental health quite detrimentally, so much so that Terry had regretted telling her about Raul's sudden appearance at their flat.

"No, mum, nobody has, and nobody will."

"I keep getting nightmares that the police are interrogating you about your involvement in the killing. I wish I could stop thinking about it, but I can't. I'm so worried, Terry."

"We're not involved and there's nothing to be concerned about, Ruth," Emily said, a tad sharply. "Let's talk about something else, shall we?"

"You'll be pleased to know," Terry said, accommodating her wish, "that our pitch to investors about the bartering platform is almost ready. The agency we're working with has identified several potential funders, and we'll be seeing them at the end of February."

"That's good to hear," Ruth said, managing a brave smile. "I remember my grandparents telling me how they would barter things all the time during the Great Depression."

"Well, we're going into another Depression now, so I suppose it's the perfect time to launch something like this."

"I actually can't believe that nobody has thought of it before," Emily remarked.

"I mean, everything in life doesn't necessarily have to involve money, does it?"

"Exactly," Ruth agreed. "Hopefully, if people start bartering and engaging with each other without cash changing hands, it'll bring them closer together. Money has the habit of coming between people."

"It certainly does," Terry said, "but I anticipate quite a few disputes arising also, especially when one of the parties doesn't follow through on their commitments, problems like that. Eventually, however, the ratings and reviews should filter out dishonest or troublesome users. That's my hope, anyway. The main utility of the platform will be allowing people to transact with one another and acquire goods and services without having to use digital currency, which is where we're going. And they'll be able to do so privately, without banks, bureaucrats, the police or the government knowing about it."

"Is the government really serious about getting rid of cash completely?" Ruth asked, shaking her head in amazement. "I can't imagine how they think we'd manage without it."

"Well, that's the plan, mum, whether we like it or not, and they're bringing forward the timeframe for implementing it. They're antsy and nervous now after what happened a few weeks ago, and an economic calamity will help them do it. We've essentially been in a recession since the beginning of the decade, but the real disaster is still ahead of us, including a run on the banks. When people can't withdraw their money anymore, then the government will pretend to be coming to their rescue and will offer full restitution, but only in a new digital currency. And they'll probably sweeten the proposition with universal basic income, or something like that. We all have to fight this. I don't want Ollie to live in a society where everything is programmable and every transaction is trackable."

Ruth nodded in solidarity. She had only recently begun to entertain the possibility that the UK government did not always act in the public's best interest.

"What *I'm* very anxious about," Emily said, "is the level of so-called 'woke' indoctrination that's taking place in our schools, and even in nurseries. Ollie will be going to one soon, and I'm terribly worried that he'll be subjected to inappropriate or even obscene performances by drag queens. There's so much sexualisation of children going on in schools right now. It's so perverted, and it's clearly orchestrated and planned from on high."

Despite being fairly liberal in her politics, Emily maintained traditional, old-fashioned views when it came to relationships and bringing up children. Terry loved the fact that their respective outlooks on such matters were so aligned. "It's nothing short of child grooming," he stated emphatically. "Transgenderism is being promoted on a massive scale as a solution to every negative feeling young people have today. They're being made to believe that changing gender will give them a leg up in life and make them happier."

"It's also a tool for population control, of course," Emily added.

"Definitely," Terry agreed.

"Isn't it the case, though, that some individuals really are born in the wrong body?" Ruth enquired.

"Of course that *can* happen, but it's very rare. Do you remember that neighbour of ours who lived just behind our house when I was growing up? His daughter and I used to play football together. She was a real tomboy. When she returned from university, she had transitioned into a man, but she—or he, I should say—never propagandised about it or pushed an agenda, he never dressed inappropriately, and he never preyed on children — or anybody for that matter. I remember seeing him in Barricade Books many years ago and thinking what a nice fellow he was. But his case was an exception. What we're seeing now is people with obvious mental illnesses and paedophiliac tendencies masquerading as the opposite sex in order to satisfy their perverted fantasies. That's totally different."

Emily sighed. "I've already told Terry that if nurseries in England go down this road, I don't want Ollie going to one at all. We'll home-school him for as long as we can."

"Absolutely," Terry said firmly. "It's all part of the globalists' transhumanism agenda, of course. First they went after the alpha males, portraying many aspects of male behaviour and responses as toxic masculinity, and now they're going after the women — the divine feminine. By making people—especially children—believe that men can be women just by identifying themselves as such, they're undermining what it really means to be a woman while also corrupting the concepts of marriage and family. Their ultimate goal is to merge humanity with AI and remove the spirit that makes each and every one of us a unique individual. To achieve this, they first have to destroy the clear binary distinction between men and women; then, when youngsters have lost all understanding of their true selves and are a confused mess, they'll be able to present their sick transhumanist concept as a panacea for everything. Once people's thought processes and behaviours start being determined by AI, then will they still be truly human? We know that millions of people have already had their DNA altered with the vaccines. We know they have nanotechnology inside their bodies. So where is all this leading? Where will it stop?"

They all stared at each other for a moment, but Emily eventually broke the silence with a hearty laugh. "My goodness, what a conversation we're having on Christmas Day! Apologies for bringing up the subject in the first place."

Terry joined her in laughter. "Indeed. Sorry for blabbering on like that. Right, let's have a lovely Christmas lunch."

*

The following day, Terry decided to take some leftover Christmas cake down to Conrad and pass on his best wishes for the coming year. He found him in a pensive mood. Conrad invited him in for a drink and poured a glass of South African Pinotage.

Terry smelt the rich, spicy aroma of the wine and complimented Conrad on his choice. After a few pleasantries, he raised the question that had been on his mind for a while.

"Conrad, I've been meaning to ask you something. How come you moved to Islington of all places, and to this particular building? You're not from around here, so was there a special reason why you chose this particular location?"

Conrad pulled out a kitchen chair and sat down. "Well, I was living in Canada with my son, but after receiving the letter about Jasmine, I wanted to return to the UK. There was no point returning to Norfolk, so I decided on London. I still have a few friends here. But finding a flat in this city isn't easy, as you know, so I turned to my employers for help."

"But didn't you leave the company years ago?"

"Yes, quite a few years ago. But in the intelligence-gathering business, once you're part of the company, you're always part of it. They don't just forget about you because you've retired."

"A bit like the CIA, then," Terry said, tongue in cheek. "So it was *they* who actually found this apartment for you?"

"That's right. Why? Is there something special about it?"

Terry didn't believe for a minute that it was pure coincidence Mia's father had been found an apartment in the exact same building where he and Emily had a flat, even though they were living in Somerset at the time. But he didn't know what it meant either. Who on earth *are* his former employers, he thought to himself. Are they somehow connected to Chimera? Were they toying with them by arranging for them to live in the same building?

"No, not at all. I'm just glad you ended up here, that's all."

"Yes, me too. Our conversations have been very satisfying, young man."

"Conrad, who exactly *were* your employers?"

"That's something I can't divulge, Terry."

*

January began with a light smattering of snow. As the days passed, Terry wondered whether Richard Andrews had forgotten about their planned meeting in London. Towards the middle of the month, he called him himself, but when he did, he found his mobile phone switched off. He tried again the following day but still couldn't get through, so he typed his domain name on his phone to see whether any messages had been placed online. To his alarm, he saw that the website was down.

He tried to make sense of the situation. In the three years he had known Richard, he had found him to be accessible at all times. On the rare occasions he had been unavailable, he had always sent out emails or posted notifications on his website to inform his friends and subscribers about his impending absence. Terry decided to post a few enquiries on Telegram to see if anybody knew anything about his whereabouts. Within an hour, he had received a dozen responses from followers of Richard's work, all saying the same thing — Richard had disappeared and his channel had been inactive since the start of the year.

Terry's heart sank. They've taken him out, he told himself. Bloody hell, they've taken him out too. Was his work on unmasking the killer of a top globalist a step too far? Wasn't bankrupting him enough? Memories of Carl's disappearance came flooding back, and Richard's words echoed in his ear — *we're all just a phone call away from being rubbed out...*

Chapter Sixteen

As January came to a close, it became all too clear to Terry that the undeclared truce between the government and the recalcitrant segment of the public was over. The government resumed its bellicose statements about pushing forward with its agenda and increased its verbal attacks on what it called 'agitators' and 'provocateurs' who it claimed were stoking up anti-government and anti-globalisation hysteria. Against this background, Terry was pleasantly surprised to see a number of prominent mainstream journalists come out strongly against the government's antagonistic stance, condemning its rhetoric and calling for dialogue and consensus-building. He wasn't sure whether these calls were genuine or whether they were part of a plan by the mainstream media to regain the public's trust, which had been severely dented by their skewed reporting of the news in the aftermath of the Downing Street killing, but he nonetheless found it interesting that such articles were being published at all.

Following the abortive protest march towards Trafalgar Square a few weeks earlier, hundreds of protestors and numerous civil rights defenders had filed lawsuits against the government for using bioweapons against peaceful demonstrators, but not a single case had come before a judge. To Terry's immense relief, Martin had recovered from the effects of these weapons, but alternative media sites were full of claims that dozens of protestors had died or were being treated for horrific injuries at specially built facilities to which their families were not being granted access.

In early February, Terry read that the UK government was about to make a major announcement in the coming days. The rumours were that it concerned the relinquishment of political sovereignty to supranational bodies and organisations. Terry wasn't convinced by the rumours, but he wasn't expecting anything positive from the announcement either. Ever since the assassination of the head of the GEC, a heavy cloud had descended not just on Britain but also on most of the West, and the sense of uneasiness and foreboding was palpable and oppressive. Both Terry and Emily felt that the Christmas period had been nothing more than a lull before the storm, and now they could clearly see the storm clouds gathering.

Surely enough, on the 11th of the month, early in the morning, it was announced that at midday the Prime Minister would be holding a press conference to outline steps that would help the country come out of the 'deep crisis' it was in. It was a Wednesday, and Emily was at home with Terry. Just before noon, they each pulled out a chair in front of the desk computer and sat down to listen.

As the Prime Minister appeared on screen, they noticed how pale and aged he looked compared to a few months earlier. His hair had gone completely white, and straggly wrinkles accentuated the look of languor and lassitude imparted by his bloodshot eyes and droopy jowl.

"He looks awful," Emily muttered. "It's like he's aged ten years in a matter of months." Terry nodded in agreement.

"It's been three months since the shocking and tragic assassination of the President of the GEC just outside this building," the speech began. "Since that abominable, terrorist act, the United Kingdom has faced a growing threat of political and financial instability, and it is incumbent on this government to restore the public's trust in the work of the bodies that formulate and implement policy for the good of the country.

"Over the last several years, it has become increasingly apparent to governments across the world that the myriad of threats and crises our countries are facing cannot be resolved fully at the national level, with individual governments acting separately and independently of each other. The terrorist act that occurred here in Downing Street has showed the world that there are many groups of people out there who are determined to subvert democracy, instil fear in the population, and undermine trust in the institutions tasked with steering policy and guiding countries through the many crises that are before us. Moreover, the internet has been usurped by unscrupulous individuals and organisations with the intention of manipulating the truth about why governments have had to resort to the measures they have taken to deal with crises such as climate change and the recent terrible pandemic. In these treacherous times, it is imperative that global solutions are found and that the bodies charged with their implementation can do so in a globally coordinated manner. It has also become abundantly clear that the effective implementation of such solutions is impeded by national politics and the inevitable political struggles that take place in the run-up to elections.

"Therefore, following extensive discussions with our global partners, as well as the Opposition and other parties across the United Kingdom, it has been unanimously decided that the only way for this country to avoid further unrest and an economic meltdown worse than that of the Great Depression of the 1930s is for key parts of our package of solutions to be implemented by supranational bodies acting above national politics and in the interests of nations and people across the globe."

Terry could hardly believe his ears. He knew instinctively what was coming next.

"To that end," the Prime Minster continued, clearing his throat, "His Majesty's Government —acting with the agreement of all the political parties represented in Parliament—has resolved to grant authority to the Global Governance Council to carry out policies in the United Kingdom that will ensure political, economic and financial stability as well as greater security for the population. These include the measures that were announced on the day of the terrorist act of last year, specifically the introduction—on the 11th of March, exactly four weeks from today—of digital identification requirements for accessing the internet, and a Bank of England digital currency to ensure the stability and integrity of the Pound. Moreover, there will be a gradual phasing out of all cash transactions exceeding £500 in order to stamp out tax evasion and allow for full transparency in all commercial as well as private transactions.

"In carrying out its duties, the GGC will be partnered with a number of global corporations, such as Chimera Inc., to ensure that the most innovative and advanced solutions can be provided. I would like to emphasise that this transfer of powers does not in any way imply a surrender of sovereignty. Just as the granting of pandemic-response powers to the World Health Organisation in 2024 ensured—without a concomitant loss of sovereignty—that our country was safer and better prepared for future pandemics, so the granting of these powers to similar supranational bodies will ensure that our country will be in a better position to address the many challenges that exist before it.

"Further details of the new measures that will be implemented in the coming months will be announced over the next few days. I call on the public to embrace these major reforms and cooperate so that the transition period can be as smooth as possible. Thank you."

Terry muted the computer and stared abjectly at the screen, shocked to his core. Emily looked at him sullenly. "They're going to turn us into modern-day slaves, aren't they?" she said eventually. "Just like Conrad said they would."

"Yes, that's what they're trying to do."

"Well, you were right about them bringing forward their agenda. They're obviously in a rush. I'm surprised they didn't announce a social credit score system as well."

"It'll come," Terry muttered solemnly. He reached for his phone to see what sort of comments were being posted on Telegram and other alternative news platforms. "Unbelievable!" he cried out after a few seconds.

"What?"

"Apparently the German Chancellor and the French President have just made almost identical speeches and have also handed over powers to the GGC."

"It's all been expertly coordinated, then."

"And the American President is expected to make a similar announcement later today..." Terry got up and moved slowly to the sofa.

"I shudder to think what's going to happen next," Emily said. "Surely there's going to be uproar. How bad do you think it'll get?" She looked at Terry, who was staring silently at the floor.

"Darling, are you okay?"

"If only Carl was here now," Terry replied softly, his voice breaking. "He'd know how to resist these measures. He'd come up with ideas on how to defeat these miscreants. If there was ever a time I needed his advice, this is it." He covered his eyes with his hand. Emily could see how affected he was emotionally but couldn't come up with the right words.

"I miss him, Em. I know it's been three years, but I still miss him."

"We all do, darling."

"Have the last few years taught people nothing? Thousands of us have spoken out about all this for years; we warned the public that the globalists would stop at nothing to achieve total control over us. And now that day is here; it's actually knocking on our door, well before their target of 2030. Have we woken up enough people? Will there finally be enough of us out there to resist? Or will we again be sidelined and ignored while the majority simply shrug their shoulders and go along with everything?"

"I really have no idea, but my gut says the elites have overplayed their hand. In their arrogance, they've gone too far, but they don't know it yet."

Chapter Seventeen

The response to the Prime Minister's speech wasn't long in coming. Within hours, reports started emerging of multiple incidents across the country where 5G cell towers had been burnt down or demolished. The media referred to these acts as criminal sabotage or arson, but Terry saw them as nothing more than justified destruction of the government's illegal surveillance infrastructure and the pulling down of a dangerous weapons system that was making people sick. He watched in amusement as many of the activists posted videos of their acts on social media. In some cases, bulldozers had been used to demolish not just the towers but also the electrical installations underneath them. In several instances, fires and small explosions had resulted at the site, causing minor injuries.

Not long afterwards, videos appeared of similar actions in Germany, France and other European countries. The determination and daring showed by the arsonists imbued Terry with a renewed hope that the globalists had indeed crossed a red line in the public's mind. He pictured himself standing at the foot of the 5G mast near their barn house in Somerset, pouring petrol around its base and igniting it from a safe distance, then watching with glee as the whole thing collapsed in a giant conflagration.

Soon, a group of activists on Telegram posted videos urging their followers to use black markers to sabotage QR code posters. Over the previous few years, these had appeared in a multitude of places across the UK, including bookshops, petrol stations and supermarkets, and companies were using them as an excuse to minimise human interaction and not accept cash. Blotting out large parts of the patterns in the matrix could crash the system, Terry found out, and this—the activists believed—would compel companies to reintroduce traditional methods of carrying out transactions. Terry decided to carry a marker with him at all times.

In the middle of the afternoon UK time, the President of the United States—looking equally sombre and morose—delivered his own surrender speech, which Terry thought sounded eerily similar to the one made by the Prime Minister. So that's it, he thought to himself. *They've* handed over sovereignty too. The world's preeminent superpower cowed into submission... Chimera must be over the moon, he grimaced.

By the evening, social media was confirming what the mainstream news outlets had already begun reporting — disruptions in internet services caused by the unprecedented arson attacks on 5G installations. Terry's neighbourhood still had internet, but he found out from friends that several parts of London did not.

"All hell's going to break loose, darling," he said to Emily during supper. "I think we're about to see what real chaos looks like."

"It was inevitable, I suppose. So many people were ignoring reality all these years, but you can't avoid the consequences of ignoring reality, can you?"

"No, you can't. Hopefully, now that millions of people will be confronted head-on with a truly nightmarish future, they'll realise they *have* to get off the fence and stop complying. This really is our last chance."

"Yes, it probably is," Emily said. "You know, in hindsight, I wish I had enjoyed my childhood so much more. Don't get me wrong, it was great. I loved growing up in Somerset with all that freedom, surrounded by beautiful countryside. But we took our freedoms for granted, as if they could never be taken away. Growing up, we just assumed that our freedoms, our privacy and our human rights would always be guaranteed. I mean, that's what World War II was all about, right? We had won the war and therefore those rights would be ours forever."

"Supposedly yes, but it turns out the post-war golden era was just a blip, a momentary lull in the plans the elites always had for us. While the immediate post-war generations were living the best years the West had ever experienced, the power-mad control-freak psychopaths were working day and night to reverse the gains ordinary people had made and to set up the structures they'd use to bring the world to its knees. It just so happens that it's *our* generation that's been called upon to fight this new war. *We* have to stop this. It's our duty. Otherwise, we'll have condemned the next generation—our children, essentially—to absolute servitude, or even worse."

"Well, you know what they say — we all choose the time and place we incarnate into. We must have *chosen* to be born when we did and to be the last generation to experience true freedom. We needed those experiences; otherwise, we wouldn't know the value of freedom. We wouldn't appreciate how important it is, and we wouldn't fight for it with such determination."

Terry looked at her thoughtfully. Emily had always been a believer in reincarnation and in the concept that humans choose the circumstances into which they are born. Prior to exploring Western Esotericism during the pandemic lockdowns, he had had little interest in such concepts, but delving into the spiritual and metaphysical aspects of human evolution had opened up a whole new world of ideas to him, and Emily's extensive knowledge in this regard had helped awaken his fascination with the topic.

"You know, when I was a teenager," he said, "I was always resentful of the fact that I'd been born at a time when the world around me was relatively boring. I'd look back at the first half of the twentieth century and be dazzled by the earth-shattering changes happening in the world at the time, especially in Europe — all those revolutions and wartime adventures. And then, I'd look at the 1990s and feel so underwhelmed by everything, so uninterested. But if you're right, it was all for a reason — I was *meant* to be born when I was, so that when this new war began, I'd be at the right age and level of maturity to be able to resist it and protect my loved ones. If I was much younger now, I probably wouldn't have been able to see through all the lies the way I did. And if I was much older, I'd probably be conditioned by the very different post-war reality and go with the crowds, like my parents did. It all makes sense."

"That's right. Don't doubt that we're living exactly in the place and time we were meant to. It was our choice."

*

The next day, Terry was amazed to see articles emblazoned across the front pages of the mainstream media condemning the granting of authority to the GGC by the world's leading countries and describing the act as a coup d'état against Western nations by the globalist elites. Far from seeking to justify the transfer of powers or to coat it with euphemistic language, the articles—many of them Op-Eds—were absolutely scathing in their attacks on the GGC, the WHO and other international bodies. These were newspapers which previously had always backed the official narrative and gone out of their way to support the government and buttress the official narrative, however ludicrous or incredible it was. Terry was astonished to see a number of them use the word 'treason' to describe what had happened. Had cracks emerged in the establishment, he wondered. Were these signs of internal dissent?

Interestingly, over the following few days, the government remained completely silent, and no further announcements were made. The only statement issued in connection with the transfer of powers was one made by the new head of the GEC, who was also the President of the GGC. In a strongly worded statement broadcast on multiple media outlets across the world, he categorically rejected the notion that there had been any surrender of sovereignty by national governments, and insisted that the only solution to the 'grave issues' confronting the world was to implement policies in a centralised and coordinated fashion, far from political intrigues and party machinations. Terry interpreted his closing words as a veiled threat — "There can be no going back now, and the means exist to ensure that."

As the new week began, social media was rife with rumours that the UK banking system was about to fold and that cash withdrawals were about to be suspended. Over the weekend, Terry had noticed large queues of people outside ATMs taking out as much cash as they could, but as Monday began, he felt a sense of panic had descended on the public. He took a drive around the neighbourhood and saw a huge crowd of people outside the local bank trying to get in. Terry and Emily had withdrawn what little money they had in their accounts upon their return to London and had bought a small safe to keep it in. As he watched the anguish on people's faces, he was torn emotionally. On the one hand, he felt empathy for the millions of people who were desperately worried about losing their money, but on the other, he felt frustration and even anger towards them for having been so lackadaisical about the government's calculated agenda all these years. Where the hell were you over the last five years, when the globalists were slowly chipping away at our freedoms, he raged at them in his head. Did it have to come to this, a run on the banks, for you to realise who your enemy was all along? As he drove back home, he tried to picture the pain that would be felt across the country if the banking system did indeed collapse. How many businesses would be forced to close down forever as a result of it? How many families would be ruined financially? He felt a sense of relief that he didn't have a small business of his own to take care of anymore.

Sure enough, the next day, late in the evening, the Bank of England announced that banks across the UK would stay shut to the public for at least a fortnight and all bank accounts would be temporarily frozen, pending a restructuring of the banking system in the face of 'structural paralysis'. In addition, cash withdrawals from ATMs would be limited to a maximum of £400 per day. As soon as Emily heard the news, she immediately thought of her brother in Frome. "This surely marks the death knell for his restaurant," she said forlornly. "He survived the stupid lockdowns and the never-ending recession, but how's he going to survive this? This situation could last months..."

"Looks like barterrealm.uk won't be getting funding any time soon either..." Terry remarked abjectly.

Emily looked at him commiseratively. "Yes, you may be right. I'm so sorry, darling. I know how hard you've worked on your idea in the last few months, but hopefully the interest will still be there when all this is over."

"Hopefully. We'll see."

*

Things accelerated dramatically from then on. Over the following week, Terry heard about dozens of banks being stormed by angry depositors, and even though the one in his neighbourhood remained undamaged, he saw videos of several other branches having their windows smashed. In one case, a branch was torched and burnt down. He also heard talk that trade unions were considering calling a general strike to demand a reversal of the government's decision to delegate authority to the GGC. He realised that the economy was sliding to a complete halt, and was glad that he and Emily had stocked up on dry foods a few weeks earlier. Supermarket shelves were bound to become empty soon, he surmised, recalling his father-in-law's premonition.

Meanwhile, a group of activists announced on social media that they were organising another massive protest in London for the 11th of March, the day on which the new measures were to be implemented. However, unlike the previous time, they gave no specific starting point or final destination, the aim being to stymie any attempt to use directed-energy weapons again. Instead, they called on people to gather wherever they could in Central London and allow the crowd's own dynamic to guide them. They stated that they were hoping for a turnout of at least three million people, a number which they claimed would be sufficient to force the government's hand. Similar large-scale protests were called for in other cities as well.

In addition to the many groups he followed on Telegram, Terry started following a new channel called NUREMBERG 2.0, on which a number of international lawyers outlined the case for citizens' grand juries to be convened to try members of parliament for treason, with some of them openly calling for citizen's arrests. Terry noticed a growing number of death threats being issued against specific MPs, and he thought it was only a matter of time before one of them was attacked and killed.

As the days wore on and the UK fell into an ever-deepening crisis, the dramatic events occurring on a daily basis started to seem increasingly surreal to Terry. Even though he had long expected the UK economy to collapse spectacularly, he still couldn't believe how suddenly and rapidly it was happening. The chaotic scenes on the country's streets mirrored those that were being seen in other countries as well, and he noted with growing alarm the spate of mass shootings and the widespread looting that were taking place in the United States, where armed militias had begun patrolling neighbourhoods in an attempt to keep them safe.

Towards the end of the month, simultaneous strikes were declared across the UK. First to strike were railway workers, who effectively brought all rail transport in the country to a standstill. Shortly thereafter, airport ground handling staff stopped working, bringing air travel to a halt and leaving millions of travellers stranded. News channels showed motorway lanes clogged with traffic as far as the eyes could see. Terry empathised with the drivers. He hated sitting in his car for endless hours, and he knew that these traffic jams were the worst ever.

Against this background, the shock waves from the closure of the country's banks were felt even more acutely. Never before had the UK experienced such a complete and long-lasting shutdown of its banking system, and the crisis was hitting ordinary households particularly badly. Terry knew that Emily was losing sleep over it, so he tried to reassure her that they would be alright, regardless of how bad things became. He opened the discussion one evening as they were sitting together on the sofa.

"I know things look really catastrophic right now," he told her calmly, "and I can only imagine how anxious you must be feeling. But I think it's important to look ahead and picture the ending we want to see. This is the chance we've been waiting for. I truly believe that, Emily. The fact that *everyone* is being hit financially now means it's only a matter of time before they see through all the lies and do something about it. As they say, it's always darkest just before dawn."

"I know, but my biggest worry is that the authorities announce a bail-in for the banks and steal everyone's money. What would happen then? Complete mayhem. Rachel called me this morning in a panicky state. She and Anthony have got £300,000 in a deposit account. If they lose it all, they'll be in a desperate plight. Anthony's not working anymore, as you know, so it's a really precarious situation for them. I felt so depressed after talking with her."

"That's understandable," Terry said gently. "Millions of people have their hard-earned income deposited in banks. The amounts are astronomical, if you think about it. But I'm trying to look at all this from a different perspective. We're close to the end, and we have to imagine a world in which these psychopaths have been crushed. We have to manifest it in our minds. Imagine what a reformed and beautiful new world we could build, given all the knowledge that's been acquired in recent years… A new kind of medicine, a new approach to education, a new system of finance, a completely new form of government. Humanity has never had such an excellent opportunity to determine its future. These really are historic times."

"I'm glad you've picked yourself up and are seeing things so philosophically," Emily said softly.

"Indeed. Have you spoken with Alan, by the way? How's he coping?"

"I spoke with him yesterday. He's keeping the restaurant closed until the situation becomes clearer. Business had plummeted anyway, he said, so there was no point in staying open and paying bills without any customers."

"He's done the right thing. We'll know what the globalists' plans are in the next few weeks, maybe sooner."

"Do you think they *will* plunder people's accounts? I mean, there's a precedent for it."

"I definitely think they were *planning* to do that, but things have changed now, what with the assassination, I mean. I think they'll try to get to their end goal sooner than planned. That's why I doubt they'll do a bail-in. More likely, they'll drag this out a bit and then offer everyone full restitution, but only in digital currency — a new Bank of England digital currency. That way they'll be able to skip forward and bring in their new financial system straight away."

"Well, if you're right, we'll know that the bank run was an engineered event too. The timing of it is just too convenient."

"Yes, and I'm sure we'll be seeing similar scenarios happening elsewhere as well. I've heard that American banks are also teetering on the edge. I wouldn't be surprised if they announce a shutdown of their banking system in the next few days."

"Terry, what do we do if they succeed in all of this? How on earth do we survive? We can't live in their open-air AI prison."

Terry took Emily's hand and kissed it. "We have to hold our nerves, darling. What's happening right now isn't just a battle between us the people and our Satanist overlords about who gets what resources to thrive on this planet; it's also a spiritual battle, and therefore we have to defeat them in our hearts and minds first. Only then, can we defeat them in the streets and on the barricades. But regardless of the outcome, we'll be okay; you, Ollie and I will be okay. Have faith, darling. There's a benevolent force out there that's protecting us; I can feel it."

"You're beginning to sound a bit like Conrad," Emily muttered with a slight grin. She had never heard him talk like that before. "Please don't quote me something from the Bible."

Terry laughed. "Well, maybe the old man knows a thing or two. I mean, look at it. What's the main underlying feature of everything sinister that's happened in our lifetime? What has the elites' agenda against humanity hinged on more than anything else? Deception. Lies. I've never been religious, you know that, but when I see how deception has been the very foundation of all the evil we've witnessed, well, it makes me wonder."

"Wonder what?"

"Whether all this really *was* written about thousands of years ago; whether we really *are* battling forces of evil that aren't from this realm. I know it sounds ridiculous, but I've been compelled by circumstances to entertain the possibility. How else can you explain an agenda to depopulate the planet and enslave the remainder of humanity?"

Emily didn't comment. She rested her head on Terry's shoulder and closed her eyes. She didn't subscribe to the idea of biblical prophesies, but in one regard she knew Terry was right. It was time to be calm and resolute.

*

As the first week of March commenced, Terry observed the chaos unfolding around them with increasing aloofness and dispassion. On Thursday morning, teachers' unions in England added to the wave of strike action and declared their own indefinite strike, effectively closing down all state schools. Close on their heels, unions representing workers in the food processing, chemicals and construction industries announced that they too would be striking as of the following Monday. That's more like it, Terry thought to himself. The oligarchs controlling the UK economy would now feel the pain, he surmised, and pressure the government to back down. He looked with satisfaction as the country showed signs of uniting behind a common cause. Despite the unprecedented economic and financial turmoil, the people he spoke to all seemed willing to endure the chaos that was unfolding around them and see things through to the end.

He was also instilled with a sense of hope that unlike the United States and many other countries, Britain was standing up and resisting the globalists relatively peacefully. A few days earlier, he had been shocked by the deadly violence that had erupted on the streets of Paris. In one incident alone, twelve people had died, eight of whom were policemen, and he had read many commentaries about how the situation in France was quickly spiralling out of control. He was encouraged by the fact that in the UK, the police seemed to be largely absent from the streets, and he noted with cautious optimism how the Commissioner of the Metropolitan Police had not made any statements, despite the dramatic developments taking place in the country. The impression Terry had was that they were sitting on the fence. If they can be persuaded to stay there, he thought, we could be in with a chance — a chance for a peaceful revolution, a very British revolution.

Chapter Eighteen

The morning of the 11th of March began with glorious sunshine. Terry awoke with a knot in his stomach. He instinctively knew that this would be one of those momentous days historians would look back on in the future as the date on which history changed course, for better or for worse. He had told Emily the day before that this time he *would* be taking part in the protest march, but he had also promised her that he would be as careful as he could and would try to stay on the periphery as much as possible. Even though she desperately wanted him not to go, she knew he was determined to be present at what he was referring to as the 'final showdown'. Martin would be joining him too, and her hope was that he would be able to spot the presence of sonic or microwave weapons well in advance and lead them both away from harm.

The protest leaders had called for people to start gathering in Central London around 1pm. Even though the government had announced the previous day that travelling between prescribed city zones anywhere in the country on the 11th would be prohibited and that fines of £500 would be imposed on anyone disregarding the ban, Terry was sure that the majority of people would ignore the restrictions. Nevertheless, he knew he would have to set off from Islington well ahead of time, given the traffic and chaos he expected to encounter along the way.

As he was drinking his morning coffee, Terry called his mother. "I just wanted to let you know that I'll be going to the protest march today. I know you'll think it's risky, but I have to go. Millions are expected to turn out, and there's always safety in numbers."

To his surprise, Ruth was fully supportive. "Yes, Terry, you absolutely must go. We've buried our heads in the sand for far too long. We've let you down. My generation has let you down. The world cannot be allowed to descend into the horrible madness they dream of. You've got to do what you've got to do, Terry. Your father would be proud of you. Just be careful, okay? I love you very much."

Terry felt a lump in his throat. Expressing such sentiments had always been a rarity in his family when he was growing up, and he had never heard his mother talk like that before. Even though he knew she had come late to the realisation that the world she was living in—a world of democracy, human rights and honest news reporting—was nothing more than illusion, she had finally made the jump. Had this realisation come sooner, she wouldn't be vaccine-injured, he believed, but he was nonetheless relieved and proud that she had succeeded in overcoming decades of programming and ingrained beliefs.

"Thank you for saying that, mum. I love you too. I'll be careful, I promise."

At 11am, just as he was about to leave to pick up Martin, a news flash appeared on his computer and he saw the words BREAKING NEWS emblazoned across the screen. An ashen-faced newsreader said that it had just been announced that the Prime Minister and the entire government had resigned with immediate effect. Terry looked with amazement as a political correspondent outside No. 10 Downing Street tried to make sense of the development. He called Martin to tell him he would be a bit late and to watch the news in the meantime. He waited to see whether the Prime Minister or the Leader of the Opposition would say anything, but neither of them released a statement or appeared before the camera. In fact, not a single member of parliament made themselves available for an interview or to answer questions, leaving commentators scrambling to explain the situation.

Terry decided to set off and listen to the news in the car. As expected, the number of vehicles at the zone's southern exit point was huge, and it took him over half an hour to get through. As he was passing over the road bumps, he saw that somebody had covered all four CCTV cameras around the checkpoint with thick plastic bags. Sometimes the best solutions are the easiest ones, he mused. He arrived at Martin's just before noon and found him waiting downstairs, listening to the news on his phone.

"You won't believe it," Martin said as he jumped in. "The Opposition MPs have resigned too, as have all the others — all 650 of them. There's nobody running the country!"

"Yes, I've just heard," Terry exclaimed, shocked and elated at the same time. "Amazing stuff. The country's in total paralysis. Ordinarily, that would be a terrifying thing, but not anymore."

"What's going on, do you think?" Martin asked.

"It's impossible to tell yet. It could be a trick, a ploy to placate the millions who are coming out onto the streets today. It does definitely look like desperation or panic, but we've been fooled before, so we shouldn't assume they're giving up just yet. Let's wait a bit and see what they do next."

They drove in the general direction of Westminster. As they came closer, the roads became chock-a-block with vehicles and throngs of people. Terry was euphoric as he observed a sea of people walking confidently and cheerfully, heading southwards towards the Thames. The mood reminded him of the jubilant crowds celebrating the end of the Second World War, but he quickly reminded himself that on that occasion victory had been declared; the situation now was far more unclear and unpredictable. These people were marching into the unknown, and there was no inkling of what could happen next.

"We're not going to be able to get any closer than this, mate," Martin said. "Park the car on the pavement, like others are doing. Nobody's going to give you a ticket today."

Terry noticed other drivers leaving their vehicles behind as well, so he found a spot where the pavement was fairly wide and parked on it. As he exited the car, a man with a loud speaker walked past, chanting WE'RE TAKING OUR COUNTRY BACK and eliciting boisterous cheers from the swarm of people all moving in the same direction. Terry looked at Martin with a huge grin. Neither of them had ever seen a crowd as big as the one they were now in. It resembled a giant wave flowing down the main streets, with tributaries joining in from the side streets.

As they got closer to Westminster Bridge, they were both mindful of the possibility that directed-energy weapons had been deployed along the routes they were taking. They assumed that if they had been, it would most likely be on the main thoroughfares rather than in the side streets. Ironically, Terry was hoping to see large numbers of policemen on the streets, believing that their presence would act as a kind of guarantee against the use of bioweapons. Disconcertingly, however, he hardly saw any. What few policemen he did spot looked calm and had smiles on their faces, and it was clear that they did not intend to impede the ever-growing crowds from getting closer to Parliament Square.

"I was expecting to see riot police, to be honest," he told Martin, a bit concerned. "Do you think they're further down, near the government buildings?"

"No idea, mate. We didn't see any last time either, if you remember. I don't know what they're up to."

They continued walking towards the river, but the closest they could get was Embankment tube station. As they stood there, Terry stared in utter amazement at the throngs of people all around them; every inch of road, pavement and green area was covered with an ocean of humanity. "There's literally millions of us here", he said to Martin, who barely heard him under the clamour of the crowds.

Just then, he bumped into the cockney commentator he followed on Telegram.

"Mick, great to see you here!" he shouted so that he could be heard. "Are you okay? I heard you got badly injured during the last protest."

"Yeah, I'm alright. Cheers. The bastards did their best to kill us, but we won't be got rid of that easily."

"What do you make of the government's resignation?"

"Like rats fleeing a sinking ship, they're trying to save their fucking skins. These cunts know what's coming."

"That's what it looks like, but it's still strange they've *all* resigned, down to the last one. Maybe they feel they'll be less vulnerable to punishment from their globalist masters if they act in unison? What do you think?"

"Maybe, and it also shows that our fucked-up leaders only have *conditional* loyalty to their masters — conditional on the satanic agenda working and them getting a seat at the table once all this bullshit is over. Now that they can see the agenda's failing and people are out for their blood, they've realised they were going to be thrown under the fucking bus. So they're all jumping ship to escape the hangman's noose, but they won't be able to, no fucking way."

Terry nodded in agreement. Martin climbed onto a granite ledge to get a better view of the Houses of Parliament in the distance. "Hopefully they're storming the building as we speak," he yelled.

"Hopefully," Terry shouted back. "It's not their building anymore, it's ours. I just hope they don't burn it down or destroy it. We'll need it."

A few moments later, loud cheers were heard from a group of people ahead of them. Terry looked towards them to see what was going on. A man pushing his way past him yelled "There's big news from America!"

Terry took his phone out of his pocket to find the news. He didn't need to search long. All the mainstream news sites had the same breaking news:

US PRESIDENT AND VICE PRESIDENT RESIGN

He couldn't believe what he was reading. He showed his phone to Martin, who raised his arms in celebration. "The bastards are running for their lives. Their masters have run out of puppets to use..."

Terry read on. According to the news flash, never in the history of the United States had there been a situation where both the President and the Vice President had resigned simultaneously. Moreover, Congressmen had been seen flying out of Washington DC, and armed militias were rumoured to be heading towards the capital to take over the White House. Blimey, he thought to himself. America's facing not just a constitutional crisis but potentially another insurrection, a genuine one this time.

"Both the UK and the US have now officially become ungovernable," he shouted out loud. He heard more and more chants and cheers as the news from America spread through the crowds. He called Emily. "Have you heard the news?" he yelled. He couldn't hear her reply due to the deafening noise around him but he could tell she was relieved to hear from him. "I can't hear you, darling, but we're okay. Don't worry. A bright, new dawn is beginning. Love you."

He hung up. This really is it, he told himself. The globalists have bitten off more than they can chew. After the millions of deaths and injuries they've caused around the world, after all the pain and suffering they've brought about, they've finally run out of accomplices. He knew they hadn't gone away yet and that they were still lurking in the shadows, but at that moment, there in the heart of London, he felt sure the tide had turned. The police were standing down, and that was good enough. The mainstream media had changed its tune. Enough people had woken up to the dark agenda. The miscreants will wither away now, he assured himself. There's nothing else they can do to us.

He remembered something Conrad had told him during one of their lengthy conversations a few months earlier. If there is a darkness growing in the world, there must be an equally growing light. Such are the laws of balance and nature.

There can only be one victor, he told himself — them or us. As he stood there, surrounded by millions of people who had finally said ENOUGH, for the first time in his life, he felt he belonged somewhere. Everything was falling into place. He was witnessing a once-in-a-lifetime event, and he was doing so with his tribe. The world was a mess, but it could be rebuilt.